OLD FLAMES,
NEW CAREERS . . .

Rob got up from the desk and lit a cigarette. Then he paced for a few moments, running his hands through his hair. "Well, first," he said, "I have to admit it's a bit of a shock to find out what it is you do for a living."

"Not respectable enough for you, Sergeant?"

"Second, this is not the kind of case that will do you any good professionally. Tony Garza is guilty of the murder of Chandler Stone, and in a very short time he'll be arrested. You'll look like a fool."

"I have to take that chance."

"And third, and I would have thought you would have given this some consideration, Caley, if you're investigating this case for my prime suspect, it won't look very good for us to be spending time together."

That one got me. . . .

MORE MYSTERIES FROM THE BERKLEY PUBLISHING GROUP . . .

MURDER BEACH

BRIDGET McKENNA

DIAMOND BOOKS, NEW YORK

This book is a Diamond original edition,
and has never been previously published.

MURDER BEACH

A Diamond Book / published by arrangement with
the author

PRINTING HISTORY
Diamond edition / December 1993

ISBN: 1-55773-967-6

Diamond Books are published by The Berkley Publishing Group,
200 Madison Avenue, New York, New York 10016.
DIAMOND and the "D" design
are trademarks belonging to Charter Communications, Inc.

PRINTED IN THE UNITED STATES OF AMERICA

10 9 8 7 6 5 4 3 2 1

CHAPTER 1

· · · · · · · · · · · · ·

THE GYMNASIUM WAS DIM AND SMELLED OF SWEAT SOCKS
and floor wax, despite lavish doses of aerosol. Someone had
lowered the lights in an effort to evoke a mood reminiscent of
high school dances gone by, but all I felt was eyestrain. In the
distance, across an expanse of worn hardwood floor that had
seemed much larger when I was seventeen, a butcher-paper
banner in purple and white spanned the back wall: WELCOME
BACK EL MORADO HIGH SCHOOL CLASS OF '77. GO, KNIGHTS.
A tape player, turned much too high for the quality of either
the tape or the speakers, was playing the top one hundred
songs of 1977, and everywhere I looked people I hardly knew
were remembering auld acquaintance without me. My new
shoes were killing my feet and my new dress was scraping
my neck and the gun in my handbag made me feel like an
utter fool.

I glanced at my watch for probably the hundredth time
and hoped I'd be out of here soon. It had been an all-day
drive down from Cascade, in the northern part of the state
to the southern California coast, for a reunion I had sworn to
avoid, and if one more old classmate came up and stared at
me blankly before reading my slap-on nametag, I was pretty
sure I'd have to scream.

"Hello, my name is Caley Burke," the tag proclaimed merri-
ly, and no, you don't know me, and you probably didn't know

1

me in 1977, either—I was the retiring redhead who always sat in the back row of every class.

I've come out of my shell somewhat over the years, but I still don't seek people out as a rule, and I don't tend to get too close to anyone. One of the reasons I enjoy working as a private investigator is the shield of profession that I can erect between myself and the people I deal with; it keeps relationships from getting too personal. Jake Baronian, my boss, was one notable exception—he insisted on being my friend. Valerie Hayden was another.

I looked around for Val in the thinning crowd. Being chair of the Reunion Committee, she was obligated to stay for most of the evening, and being her best friend and not having had the foresight to bring my own car, so was I.

I hoped my being here really meant a lot to Valerie, because there probably wasn't another person on earth I would have done this for. When she had called me yesterday, close to tears, and begged me to come down right away, I hadn't even been able to come up with a good excuse. I knew Jake would give me the time off, and the bonus he had just given me for wrapping up a long and difficult insurance case would more than cover the new wardrobe that would make me feel up to facing the old crowd in Morado Beach.

Valerie wouldn't discuss the problem in detail, only that her grandfather was in some kind of trouble, but there would be plenty of time to talk about it—I promised her I'd come for a week. She was very close to her grandfather, and she sounded terribly worried about him. She also sounded like she needed a friend, and with my tendencies toward hermithood it was largely through Val's efforts that our friendship had survived five hundred miles and fifteen years. I owed her something for that.

I felt a hand on my shoulder, and paused for half a second to summon up the grace for a polite conversation with yet another divorced football star who hadn't had the time of day for me fifteen years ago. I turned around to face the latest, and my face froze halfway to the strained smile I had been preparing.

"Hi, Caley."

"Rob." All the thousands of things I had once prepared to say if I ever saw Rob Cameron again were locked away in some forgotten compartment of my mind, and all I could do was repeat myself. "Rob."

"Dance?" He held out his arms and I moved forward and we were out on the dance floor. I remembered as surely as if no time had passed how it felt to be fifteen and in love with a boy who had never noticed me; to be sixteen and his pal, listening to him talk about how the girl he was in love with this week wouldn't give him the time of day; to be seventeen and have him finally start noticing me, taking me out, kissing me into delirium, making love to me in backseats and borrowed apartments, and having my heart broken when his long-lost gorgeous homecoming queen came back around declaring her undying infatuation. In three seconds I ran the gamut between sweet nostalgia for the good old days and the sensation of being elbowed in the solar plexus.

"I was hoping you'd be here," he was saying. If he had said anything before that, it hadn't penetrated the fog.

I made myself stare into those smoky green eyes and play it cool. I shrugged as though it were no big deal. "I wasn't planning to be. It was a last-minute decision."

"I know. Valerie told me she'd asked you to come. I'm glad you did. It's been an awfully long time, Caley."

Mercifully, the song ended before I had to figure out what to say to that. "I think I'd like something to drink" was what I managed, and it was pretty cliché, but so was the punch bowl in the corner brimming with pinkish liquid and half-melted chunks of ice. Cliché is what high school reunions are all about.

Rob poured me a paper cup of the punch and we stood and watched the dancers.

"Still living up north?" he asked.

"Yes. I like it there. Not a beach in sight." I could hear myself being flip; I faced away from him, pretending to watch the dancers.

Rob moved back into my line of sight. "You've never come back to visit." The green eyes pinned me, demanding a degree of sincerity.

"I thought about it a lot of times. Val and I usually meet for a weekend in San Francisco or L.A. a few times a year. My parents sold the house, and there wasn't anything I needed to come back for."

He seemed to think that part over, wondering if I was being general or specific. He took a step closer, leaned against the table. "You know, I've thought about driving up there some time and dropping in on you."

"I'm glad you didn't. I hate surprises." I was still having trouble meeting his eyes. I made an effort to look at him. He was good to look at, without being classically handsome—tall and well built, with straight brown hair that tended to fall down on his forehead, so that I was even now resisting the urge to brush it back.

"I guess your life is all settled up there, huh?" He put down his cup and picked up my hand. "No room for old high school sweethearts in your present arrangement?"

I could feel my face taking on the pink flush that all redheads abhor. It was pretty dark; maybe he wouldn't notice. "I try not to think of anything as settled," I said, looking up at him with my "confident professional woman" look. "It usually turns out to be bad luck. But yes, I like my life." That much was perfectly sincere.

"Well, I'm just glad you're back. Will you be in town long?"

"A week. I'm staying at Irene Hayden's place." Valerie's mother was out of town, and Val, her husband Russ, and their kids were spending a couple of weeks there while they waited for their house to be remodeled. It would be a real vacation, the first I'd had in years, and I realized how much I was looking forward to it.

"I was thinking maybe we could get together—have some lunch, go to dinner at the Seaside, sort of like old times. Would you like that?"

Rob had never taken me to the Seaside, of course. In those days he could scarcely afford burgers and fries, but he'd managed to scrape up enough to impress Melissa Meredith into bed, and into marriage soon after I had fled town. Well, that was all a long time ago, wasn't it? And the truth was, I was just as attracted to Rob Cameron this minute as I had been at seventeen.

"It sounds great. Call me at Irene's."

He pulled a card case out of his jacket pocket. "I may be pretty busy the next couple of days. If you haven't heard from me by tomorrow night, call me. If I'm not there, call the other number. That's my house."

He handed me his card. At the top was the embossed seal of the City of Morado Beach, featuring sandpipers and freeway overpasses. In the middle was the logo of the Morado Beach Police Department. At the bottom it read: Robert L. Cameron, Detective Sergeant. I hoped my eyes hadn't widened noticeably. Despite the fact that his father had been on the force, of all the things I ever pictured Rob Cameron doing for a living, being a policeman wasn't one of them.

"Thanks." I opened my bag carefully a fraction of an inch and deposited the card between a tube of Misty Peach lip gloss and my Walther PP .32 caliber pistol. "I'll do that."

I looked across the room and saw Val saying good-bye to a mutual acquaintance. She looked as much like a Greek goddess as ever, with thick dark hair falling down her back in perfect waves, and a serenely beautiful face on a knock-out body.

I wear my hair short because I can't figure out what the hell to do with it, and no one has ever described me as a goddess. In high school I used to wonder why Val wanted to be seen with me, but I finally figured out she just plain liked me. It was enough then, and it still was fifteen years later.

A moment later Val was coming toward us, jacket over one arm, and I guessed it was finally time to go. Part of me regretted not being able to bask in Rob's attentions a bit longer, but the sensible part knew it was time to make my exit. "Always leave them wanting more" isn't only applicable to show business.

"Hi, Val. I guess you've come to steal Caley away from me."

"Hello, Rob." Val barely looked at him. There was a certain tension in her voice. Something was going on here I knew nothing about, and I was curious. She turned to me. "Would it be all right if we left now? I don't think I can take another minute of this." She indicated the surroundings with an exhausted gesture.

"That's what I've been thinking for two hours. I can't wait to get out of these shoes. Rob, I guess I'll be seeing you again before I leave town."

He put a hand on my shoulder. "Bank on it. Let me walk you two ladies out to your car."

We pushed open the ancient gym doors and stepped outside. The onshore breeze had cooled the evening down considerably after a warm late-spring day. Rob put his arm around my shoulders and I was grateful for both the warmth and the contact. Val walked ahead to her car, giving us some space.

It was an unreal feeling, seeing him again after all these years, and even more unreal to have this show of interest. All the months after he left me for Melissa, when I had waited for him to come find me, and all the years in between paled beside a simple walk across a parking lot.

We stopped beside Val's Mazda, and he leaned down and kissed me. "I'll talk to you tomorrow." He turned and walked back toward the gym. I slid into the bucket seat and fastened my seat belt with hands that shook just a little.

My head was spinning with possibilities. Maybe we could pick up where we left off, I told myself. Maybe he knew he had made a mistake, I told myself. Maybe he knew he should never have given me up.

"Are you going to close the door?" Val asked with just a touch of sarcasm.

"Of course. I was just going to do that." I closed it.

"Right." She shook her head. "Check to see if your head's screwed on, and let's get the hell out of here."

CHAPTER 2

IRENE HAYDEN'S HOUSE WAS A THREE-STORY, ELEVEN-ROOM, Spanish-style mansion on its own stretch of private beach about ten minutes north of town. Valerie had grown up here, benignly neglected by her mother and only acquainted in passing with her father, whose engineering business kept him traveling most of the year.

She and her brother David, who was a year older than us, had turned to their grandfather early on for the affection they missed at home—and they had to sneak to do that. Irene hated her father and would not acknowledge their relationship; Antonio Garza was Mexican and she could never forgive him for that.

Irene would be out of town this week, and even though Val and Russ were staying there while their house was being remodeled, they would seldom be around, and I would have the run of the place—an idea that pleased me. When Valerie and I spent time here when we were in school together, I would find myself fantasizing that it was my house, and that I would never have to move. My family had a tendency to pick up and move once a year or so; my two years in Morado Beach was the longest stretch I ever lived anywhere until I got to Cascade the year after graduation, where I put down both feet and refused to leave. I've been there ever since.

Valerie's car pulled up to the head of a long curving drive-way, where my frightfully middle-class Subaru thumbed its nose at the elegant surroundings. She killed the engine. "So what was it like seeing Rob again?"

I shook my head. "Words fail. It was great, it was painful, it was confusing. . . ."

"Are you thinking about getting something going again?"

"Well, that takes two, doesn't it?"

"Rob certainly seemed interested. I was wondering if you were."

I thought about it, but not for long. "Until an hour ago, I'd have said I wasn't interested. Absolutely not. No way. Then I saw him again and it all came back to me. It was almost as though no time had passed at all."

"Only fifteen years. I guess I just want you to be careful."

"I think we've both grown up a lot since high school."

Valerie sighed and smiled at me. "Then I guess it deserves a chance. Let's get you settled into a room and I'll make us a drink. Then we can talk."

She grabbed my bags and I followed her up the stone walk to the front door. "God, I'm glad you came, Caley," she said as she unlocked the door. She pulled a spare key off the ring and pressed it into my hand. "The last few days have been utter hell."

We walked across an expanse of terra-cotta entranceway that was bigger than the living room of my apartment, and up a winding staircase right out of a movie about the rich and famous of southern California. I had always loved that staircase—it only needed Jean Harlowe in a white satin dress descending in candlelight. What it had was me ascending in green rayon with my shoes in my hands and my handbag bumping against my hip at each step.

"Do you mind staying in my old room? It's closest to the stairs."

"Sounds perfect. I can't wait to get out of this outfit. Tell me again why women wear panty hose."

"I'm not sure, but I think it might be a plot on the part of the women's wear industry." She opened the door to the room and switched on the light. "If you didn't bring anything to relax in, we could see what's in Mom's closet."

"That's okay, I brought my favorite ratty robe—I'll be right at home once I get into it."

"You do that. I'll go raid the liquor closet." She laughed and shook her head. "It's been a while since we did that."

I remembered it very well. "Sixteen years. You got so shit-faced I had to put you in a hot bath and feed you coffee."

Val shook her head. "It didn't help, but at least you got me safely into bed before I passed out." She swung the two suitcases up onto the bed.

"And at least Irene didn't come home until I accomplished it." I laughed, remembering. "You were so sick the next day, I couldn't enjoy my own first hangover. Let's show some restraint this time, okay?"

"It's a deal. See you downstairs. I've got a favor to ask, so brace yourself."

Ten minutes later I descended the staircase, not quite Jean Harlowe in my robe of worn white terry cloth adorned with pulled threads. I walked into the living room where Valerie had started a fire and drawn the heavy drapes against the draft from the seaward windows, but the sound of the surf outside made a chill pass through me. This close to the ocean, the air is always damp, and a fine moisture permeates everything. The nights, even in summer, are cool.

I picked up the rum on the rocks Valerie had fixed me and then I snuggled up on the end of an eight-foot velvet sofa closest to the fire. Valerie sat down on the other end and kicked off her shoes, drawing her feet up under her. She folded her arms close about her chest. There was a stiffness about her that seemed unusual to me.

"So what's up, Val? What's happening with Tony?" I had guessed the problem with her grandfather was serious—she hadn't written in over a year, and for Val that was unthinkable.

She took a swallow of her drink. "There was a fire in his studio. He was burned over sixty percent of his body."

I felt the stab in the pit of my stomach that I always feel when I hear something like that. "Is he okay now?" My hand clutched my abdomen in a reflex I was only aware of after I had done it.

"He was in the hospital almost a year, but he's been out about a month now. David's there to take care of him, but you know Tony. He likes to do things for himself. But it's hard. And he hasn't painted since the fire."

Antonio Garza was one of the best-known painters of Southwest themes in the country. Valerie owned an art gallery in town where she displayed his work. He had made a happy life for himself without a wife or his daughter, who ignored him if she passed him on the street in town. His grandchildren loved him, and he had his art, and he kept a lot of bored Morado Beach wives happy over the years, and went on the occasional roaring drunk. He had always been friendly and kind to me, and it distressed me to hear of his suffering.

"I'm so sorry. It must have been awful for him. And for you."

"Yes. It's been a terrible year." She finished the drink and got up to make another. Her hands shook noticeably as she went through the automatic motions of ice and liquor.

"You said Tony was in trouble. That's about something else, isn't it?" I got up and brought my glass over for some more ice, mainly to have something to do.

"The night before I called you, a man was murdered here in Morado Beach. No one you knew. A man who only came to town a few years ago. His name was Chandler Stone." Valerie's voice began to break. She blinked back tears. "Tony is a suspect. The police think he may have killed Chandler."

That explained the tension between Valerie and Rob earlier that evening. "They haven't arrested him, have they?"

She shook her head, eyes closed against tears. "Not yet. But I think they might soon."

"Valerie, you're not saying you think he did it?"

"I don't know." Her voice was choked. She walked back to the sofa and sat silently for a minute or more, staring at the fire. "He could have, I think," she said finally, meeting my eyes. "He hated Chandler. Earlier in the week they had an argument in front of another man. Tony threatened to kill Chandler then."

I picked up my glass, the ice forgotten. "I know Tony's got a reputation for being hot-tempered, but Jesus, Val, we're talking murder here. Do you honestly think he's capable of that?"

"I think he might be, but I just don't know. Caley, I feel awful saying that—even thinking it—but he did threaten to, and I can't think of anyone else who would want to kill Chandler." Tears rolled down her cheeks, streaking her face. "I don't know what to do, or who to turn to except you."

It was my turn to guzzle an ounce of rum. I shuddered and poured a refill. Valerie was getting herself back together. I wished I could offer more comfort, but I'm lousy in these kinds of situations.

I let several automatic questions pass without asking them: When, where, and how was Stone murdered? Did Tony have an alibi for the time of the murder? Who else in town did Chandler Stone have dealings with?

It wouldn't take a rocket scientist to figure out what the favor was that Val wanted from me. I had been working as an assistant investigator to Jake Baronian up in Cascade for the past three years, and was now a licensed private investigator.

The problem was, although working for friends was fairly common in my business, it still wasn't an idea I was comfortable with. Trying to keep my best friend's grandfather out of jail on a murder charge when even she wasn't certain of his innocence sounded like a giant pain in the ass for a fledgling P.I. with a brand-new license and my own quota of insecurity.

I sat back down on the couch. "You want me to take the case, don't you?"

She managed a smile. "For a woman who's always billed herself as shy, you can be awfully direct sometimes."

"I learned it at Jake Baronian's knee. You want me to take the case? You want me to get some of the heat off Tony? I'll be even more direct, Val, I don't really want to do it. I haven't got much experience in felony investigations. What if he goes to jail because I'm not up to the job?"

"If you don't take the case, he's almost certain to go to jail anyway. We need help."

"There are probably a dozen private investigators between here and San Diego with the right kind of experience."

"You're the one I want."

I set my glass down on the coffee table. "Listen to yourself, Val—you're asking your dental assistant to perform your brain surgery."

"Stop. Let's not argue about it—we'll let Tony decide. We can go see him tomorrow. I don't think we have much time, Caley. Just promise me you'll talk to him."

"All right. I'll talk to him." What could it hurt? Besides, I liked Tony. He was one of the good memories I still had about this town.

"And if he wants you to take the case you will?"

I discovered I wasn't capable of refusing straight out, much as I was tempted to do just that. "If he asks me to do it, I'll do it. But I'm going to talk to him first and lay all this on the line."

The look of relief on Val's face was almost worth the discomfort I was going through. "Thank you, Caley. I have to warn you about something, though. He's terribly burned."

"It's okay. I have a pretty good idea what to expect." And I did, but I couldn't say I was looking forward to it.

We sat there a little while longer, drinking and watching the fire die down. The ocean pounded relentlessly at Irene's stretch of beach. Finally, Valerie set down her drink. "I have some newspaper clippings upstairs; articles about . . . the shooting. Would you like to read them?"

"Not tonight. I haven't been hired yet, remember?"

"It can wait till tomorrow, then. God, look at the time. I've got to get to the gallery first thing in the morning. I guess I'd better be getting to bed, how about you?"

"Sure. You can walk me to my room." I finished my drink. "I'll be asleep in five minutes."

An hour later I was still staring at the painted plaster ceiling of Val's old room. I had begun by remembering the times we had spent roaming the house and grounds during the two years I lived in Morado Beach—the time we threw a party when Irene was out of town, the time we nearly drowned in a narrow cave in the cliff wall when the tide came in.

From there I remembered school, and Rob, and Val's brother David, who was easily the best-looking boy in school when I was a junior and he was a senior. I would catch him looking at me down a hallway or across the cafeteria, and like every other girl in school, I would hope he wanted to take me out.

Like a lot of other Anglo girls in school, I knew what my parents' reaction would be. David didn't look Mexican, with his fair skin and deep blue eyes, but he had a Mexican grandfather, and Anglo girls from "better" families didn't date Mexican boys in Morado Beach in 1975, especially if they had to defy their parents to do so, and I had certainly not been an exception to that rule. I closed my eyes on remembered days, and a vague regret followed me to sleep.

CHAPTER 3

I WOKE UP AT 7:00 A.M., A HABIT I DEPLORE ON A WEEK-
end, but instead of rolling over and going back to sleep for
an hour, I dragged myself into the shower. Val had said she
would leave for the gallery about 5:30, but she would be back
before 8:00 to take me over to Tony's house. I needed to feel
human when I faced him. A shower and some coffee should
accomplish that.

I felt terrible for what Tony had gone through, and it was
that as much as anything that made me determined not to
jump into the case. He deserved an experienced investigator.
My credentials consisted of three years of background checks,
a handful of insurance fakers and marital stakeouts, and half a
dozen runaway locates—not exactly Sam Spade.

I wrapped my old robe around me and walked barefoot
downstairs into the kitchen to put on some coffee. There was a
bag of Jamaica Blue Mountain in the cupboard; nothing but the
best for Irene, just like always. It smelled heavenly brewing as
I hung my head down and brushed my hair. The kitchen door
opened. "Yeah, I know I'm not dressed yet—you're lucky I'm
not standing here naked."

"I'm not sure about that," a man's voice replied, and my
head snapped up.

David Hayden had grown up right along with Val and I, but
I hadn't been expecting it, somehow. He was as difficult not

14

to stare at at thirty-three as he had been at seventeen, with those impossible blue eyes. The obligatory south coast morning fog had caused his dark hair to curl just a bit along the side of his neck, and he was grinning at my discomfiture. I forced my mouth closed. "I guess I don't have to say it wasn't you I was expecting," I ventured.

"No, I guess not. And I should have knocked. I'm sorry. Maybe it was coming around back that made me feel like I lived here again. I don't visit Irene that often. Val asked me to come over and pick you up."

I shrugged, more casually than I would have thought possible. "Pour yourself some coffee if you like. I'm going to get dressed." My heart was beating miles a minute as I raced upstairs and checked out my new wardrobe for my best "going for a drive with an old not-quite boyfriend" outfit.

When it had finally happened, when he finally stopped me walking across the lawn between classes and asked me to go to a movie with him, I turned him down, as I always feared I would, but I told him why—I figured I owed him that. "My father wouldn't let you in the door if you showed up to take me out," I told him. "I'm sorry. I really would like to go out with you. I just can't." And he nodded as though he were expecting it, and he said, "That's okay, Caley. I understand," as though he meant it.

He would stop and talk to me a lot after that, and sometimes just happen to be where I was hanging out after school and buy me a Coke and sit and talk for a while. Meanwhile, girls with similarly prejudiced parents who were willing to sneak out had dates with him, and I wondered if I had done the right thing.

David didn't forget about me, though, and instead of dating we became friends. I took to hanging out at Tony's house with him and Val. He took me on sketching trips up and down the coast, with Val always along to keep my folks happy, and he helped me improve my drawing. I always wanted to be better to please him.

He was there through the whole Rob thing, and the Rob and Melissa thing, but when I finally got dumped I was too ashamed to burden him with my broken heart. When that happened, I shut him and everyone else out of my life. My parents picked up and moved again right after that, and I was relieved to be able to turn my back on the town and everyone in it.

In the fifteen years since I left Morado Beach I had heard news of David's life—he was a successful painter in his own right these days—and I had seen pictures of him that Valerie brought to our weekends in the city. But this was the first time we had seen each other.

It would definitely have to be the turquoise shirt and black jeans for this occasion, I decided, and a touch of lip gloss. I checked out the final product and decided it would have to do, grabbed some sandals out of my suitcase and carried them down to the kitchen.

David handed me a mug of coffee. "Black okay? You want to take it along or drink it here?"

I didn't feel like I knew what to say over coffee. Better to get right down to the business at hand. "I can drink it in the car—let's go."

"We've been out of touch for a while, haven't we?" David said, breaking the awkward silence that had formed between us as we drove down the coast highway toward Tony's.

"That's my fault," I said. "I'm sorry it took an emergency to get me back to Morado Beach. I won't let it happen again."

"So you're a private investigator." He turned his head to smile at me. "You don't look the part somehow."

"Well, I left my trench coat back in my office when I drove down here yesterday."

"And the bottle of cheap Scotch?"

"It's in my desk drawer next to the fedora and the crumpled pack of cigarettes. I'm a real stickler for tradition."

David laughed. "It's good to see you again, Caley."

It was good to see him, too. I hadn't forgotten David's friendship, but like so many things and so many places, I'd put it behind me and kept myself from looking back. I'd given up moving from place to place, but evidently I hadn't stopped running away.

Tony's house was on the other side of town, a block inland from a public beach teeming with surfers in vivid wet suits out beyond the breakers. We parked David's pickup behind Valerie's car and walked up toward the house.

I tried to broach the subject of my uncertainty again, but David shook his head. "We'll let Tony decide. Val has a lot of faith in you, you know."

"Yes, I do know, but that doesn't mean it's well placed."

"Doesn't mean it isn't," he said, giving me a sidelong look.

Antonio Garza's house was small and charming in contrast to the imposing presence of his daughter's beach mansion, and commanded a nice view of the Pacific without being right on the coast highway. It was painted the blue of a desert sky and surrounded by an overgrowth of bright flowering plants—bougainvillea twining between a fence and a grape arbor, red and golden poppies growing under and between shaggy shrubs that had once been a hedge. This was the house he had lived in when Irene was just a little girl, and even when he had become a well-known and respected artist—and certainly well paid—he had never moved from this place.

There was a wooden swing on the porch, weathered silver-gray from sun and salt. It made a creaking sound in the morning breeze that took me back with an aching suddenness to the last time I had been here, in happier times. The door stood open behind a screen, and the room beyond was dark.

David held the screen door open and I walked in ahead of him. Valerie was sitting in a big chair with her feet drawn up under her, petting a battle-scarred black tomcat. She gave me a little wave as I came in.

The curtains were drawn. The figure seated on the couch was in shadow, but it was easy to recognize Tony's trademark white shirt and pants, the gold-headed cane. The commanding presence of Antonio Garza was unmistakable. I walked toward the couch and extended my hand, bracing myself for the scars I knew would be there. He rose, gripping the head of the cane, until his face was level with mine.

It was so much worse than I had expected. There was no nose, no ears, a swollen slit for a mouth. The eyes were raw scars in a twisted landscape of tissue. What had once been Antonio Garza's face was blowtorched beyond recognition into a contorted parody of human features. There was evidence of skin grafts, but no amount of reconstruction could have availed against the injuries I saw. I could find no trace of the handsome Mexican gentleman who served lemonade on the porch on summer afternoons when I would visit with Valerie and David, the man whose charm and virility were legend among other men's wives on a thirty-mile stretch of southern California coastline. This was something alien.

My head jerked slightly as I set my muscles against turning away. I fought my instinctive reaction to bolt for the door and forced myself to break the silence that was stretching between us like glass wire.

"Mr. Garza. It's been a very long time."

"Yes, it has. Valerie tells me you are here because of my problem. She worries too much about me. David, too. Won't you sit down?" He motioned to David. "Get our guest some coffee, *hijo*. Where are your manners?"

I took a seat on a leather hassock across from Tony's couch, and Tony sat down after me. A grizzled terrier of uncertain lineage jumped up on the couch and put his head on Tony's leg. Tony patted the dog and spoke to him in Spanish. The terrier picked up one of the black leather gloves that were lying next to Tony's leg and began to play with it, whipping his head back and forth and growling in a ridiculous little tenor voice. "Bad dog," Tony chided him, removing the glove from his mouth and swatting him gently on the nose. "Very bad."

David winked at me over his grandfather's head and went into the tiny kitchen. He returned with a steaming mug of black coffee, which I grasped gratefully. The little motions that surrounded something as familiar as a cup of coffee were very comforting to me in their utter familiarity right then.

I looked above the couch where a portrait of Tony hung in a simple oak frame. It showed a handsome olive-skinned man with silver hair and laughing black eyes. It held the soul, the personality of the man in front of me. It was signed D. Hayden.

"Valerie says the police may think you killed a man," I began.

He nodded thoughtfully. "It's possible that they do. I did say I was going to kill him, and perhaps I would have, too, but someone else beat me to it."

"Valerie has asked me to investigate the case and try to take some of the suspicion away from you, hopefully even to find the real murderer. I am an investigator, but I've never handled a case of this importance. I have to tell you that I think you'd be better off turning the case over to an established detective with more of the right kind of experience. I can find you one, if you like."

Tony turned to David and spoke in rapid Spanish. David replied. I couldn't catch a word of their exchange. Not for the first time, I regretted not learning it in school. My two years of French qualified me to read menus in restaurants I couldn't afford to eat in, but a knowledge of Spanish would have come in handy a hundred times over.

Tony switched to English as he turned back to me. "Why do I need a stranger poking into my business? You're a friend— I've known you since you were a girl. You know I like the ladies, and that I drink too much sometimes, and that my daughter doesn't speak to me on the street in town. I am not embarrassed by this because I feel you are almost family. No." He shook his head. "No, I don't want a stranger coming around and dissecting my life like a prize bug. If Valerie and David think we must have someone investigate the death of this pig Chandler Stone, then we will. But not a stranger." He set the tip of his cane against the floor in front of him with a slight thump, as though to settle the matter once and for all.

I sipped at my coffee for a moment, and forced myself to look back up. I met David's eyes over Tony's head, and he nodded. It seemed I was overruled. "All right, Mr. Garza. If it's what you want, I'll take the case. You understand that I'll have to ask you a lot of questions about your relationship to Chandler Stone and about the argument between you. It's important that I have all the facts."

Tony stared straight ahead as though I had not spoken. I thought perhaps his mind was elsewhere, and I repeated my request for information, a little louder.

"I am not deaf, *niña*, I am simply not going to discuss it."

"But, Mr. Garza, it's important to your case for me to know as much as I can about these things. Surely the police have spoken to you about this?"

"They have spoken to Valerie and David, to Valerie's husband, even. And yes they have asked their questions of me— the same ones you want to ask, I'm sure. But I have not answered. They told me I could have a lawyer present. I don't need a lawyer."

I wondered how he had stayed out of jail this long, and decided he must have a hell of an alibi. I tried again. "I understand how the police can be about these things; they're suspicious of everyone, and sometimes unpleasant. But I'm here as your friend. Believe me, I can't do this investigation justice without some information from you."

"Please, Tony," Valerie pleaded, getting up from her chair and coming over to us, "this is to keep you out of jail."

"I will not speak of this thing any further. I did not shoot that bastard Stone and the police will find this out with your help. David and Valerie can tell you anything you need to know." He rose from the couch, leaning heavily on the cane, and walked out of the room and down the narrow hall to his bedroom, the little dog at his heels. He went into the room and shut the door behind him.

I looked between Valerie and David in shock. "I have to have his cooperation. I can't conduct an investigation without some input from him. He's my client; he's the whole *point* of the investigation."

"Tony's been very strange since the fire," Valerie said. "Some people say it made him insane."

"Some people say he was crazy before the fire," said David. "He's an artist, an eccentric, and, let's face it, sometimes a drunk. He always had a reputation for copping an attitude that no one else could understand, so he must be crazy, right?" He got up and paced between his chair and the door, stopping finally to stand and look at the ocean through the screen.

I caught myself staring at David too long, so I got up and put my coffee cup down on the mantelpiece. I looked up at the two portraits of David and Val that Tony had painted when they were teenagers. Besides Tony's portrait over the couch, they were the only pieces of art in the room. "Is there any chance—any chance at all in your opinion—that Tony could actually have killed Chandler Stone?"

"I honestly don't know," Valerie said in a very small voice. She sat back down in the chair, looking small and tired.

I turned around. David's eyes were boring into me angrily. "My grandfather is not a murderer. He's a broken old man whose life has been burned away—an artist who'll never paint again. He may even be crazy, but he didn't kill anybody. I don't think I care much for you falling back into our lives after fifteen years and deciding you know more about him than I do. Maybe you never really knew any of us."

The words hurt, but I tried not to react to them. "I'm sorry, David—I wasn't accusing him. I just had to know what you thought."

"I think it would be helpful to him if you believed he was innocent." He left the room.

"Well, shit, I blew that one." I went to sit across from Valerie. My legs were shaking, and there was a lump of hurt feelings in my throat. "But how am I going to investigate without being able to ask David questions or interview your grandfather?"

"I'll speak to Tony. I think maybe I can wear him down. And don't worry about David. He's just so goddamned sensitive where Tony's concerned—so protective."

"And now he feels like he's got to protect him from me. So far this is going worse than I expected. Would you mind giving me a lift back to Irene's? I need to get my car and do some running around. I'll need those newspaper articles you mentioned last night. Mainly, I just don't want to be here when David comes out."

CHAPTER 4

· · · · · · · · · · · · · · ·

AFTER SPENDING A WHILE WITH VALERIE'S NEWSPAPER CLIP-
pings, my next stop was the Morado Beach Police Department.
It would be awfully handy to be able to get a look at the police
reports on the Chandler Stone murder, but I had a good idea
what my chances were of getting Rob to let me see anything
on an active case—police traditionally regard P.I.s as amateurs
meddling in their business, and they're not always wrong. I
couldn't expect Rob to bend the rules for me, but he might
be willing to part with some general information I hadn't been
able to get out of the newspaper. At the very least, I had to tell
him about my involvement in the case.

The Morado Beach City Center was as trendy as any shopping center in town, situated on an ocean-view lot a few blocks
from the beach, and sporting the red tile and pink stucco that
had taken over the whole look of the south coast of late.
Palms and palmettos were scattered here and there among
strategically located boulders, and a terra-cotta walkway led
up to a terra-cotta atrium from which sprouted half a dozen
office doors, one reading "Police Department, City of Morado
Beach."

I walked in and faced a bored desk officer in a spotless khaki
uniform and high-tech headset, who had been catching her soaps
on a tiny television. Her tag identified her as HOGAN.

"I'm here to see Detective Sergeant Cameron."

22

A frown line appeared between Hogan's eyebrows. "You're not with the press, are you?" She jerked her head to indicate a group of people waiting expectantly along one wall, several of them armed with video cameras and battery packs, the rest with notebooks and mini tape recorders. Obviously, the latest small-town murder story had not yet run out of steam.

"No, I'm a friend."

"Is he expecting you?"

"Yes." That was stretching the truth, but I'd gotten good at that the past three years. It came in handy for getting information and cooperation from strangers.

She punched up two digits on the phone. "Your name, please?"

"Caley Burke."

"Sergeant Cameron, Ms. Burke is here to see you; shall I send her in?" she said. "Thank you. Go back to the second door on the left. Sergeant Cameron will see you." She was back in soapland before I could take two steps. A door on the right opened, and two men stepped out, conversing in low tones.

I kicked myself mentally for being too preoccupied to check my hair before I got out of the car, and I'd be damned if I would do it in front of someone. I'd just better look good enough. I walked up to Rob's door and knocked.

"Come in," Rob said, then "Hi!" when he saw me. He stepped out from behind the desk and took a pile of papers off the nearest chair so I could sit. "I tried calling you at Irene's this morning, but there was no answer. You must have read my mind; I was going to ask you to lunch at L'Auberge."

L'Auberge was the fanciest and stuffiest place in town. I thanked myself for changing before I left Irene's the second time, and for choosing something slightly dressy. "Lunch sounds great, but I'm also here on business."

"Well I'll be damned." He leaned against the corner of the desk and looked down at me with wry amusement. "You've been in town less than a whole day, and you're already in trouble with the law."

"Not exactly, but Tony Garza is."

He cocked his head. "Don't think me rude, but what business is that of yours?"

I took a deep breath and leaned forward. "Rob, has Valerie ever mentioned what it is I do for a living?"

"Not on her own, but when I asked her, she said you work for a lawyer. I guess I assumed you were a legal assistant or something." He frowned. "Is that what you are?"

"Not exactly. I do work for a lawyer; his name is Jake Baronian. Only he doesn't practice law anymore. He's a licensed private investigator."

"And what does that make you?"

"For the first three years I worked for him, I was an assistant in his agency. A couple of months ago I got my license."

"You're trying to tell me you're a P.I. and Tony Garza's asked you to come in on this case." It was impossible to read the expression on his face, though I gave it my best.

"Actually, Valerie and David asked me. I don't think Tony cares if anyone investigates it."

"Christ, Caley, don't do it! Turn them down."

"Too late for that, Rob—I already told Valerie I'd take the case."

"Then tell her you've changed your mind. If she's given you any money, return it. Just don't do this."

He was beginning to piss me off. "I don't think I understand why you're so vitally concerned about what cases I take."

Rob got up from the desk and lit a cigarette. Then he paced for a few moments, running his hands through his hair. "Well, first, I have to admit it's a bit of a shock to find out what it is you do for a living."

"Not respectable enough for you, Sergeant?" I shot back. He ignored me.

"Second, this is not the kind of case that will do you any good professionally. Tony Garza is guilty of the murder of Chandler Stone, and in a very short time he'll be arrested. You'll look like a fool."

"I have to take that chance."

"And third, and I would have thought you would have given this some consideration, Caley, if you're investigating this case for my prime suspect, it won't look very good for us to be spending time together."

That one got me. Of course it was fairly obvious that Rob was interested in seeing me, maybe even in starting up where we had left off so many years ago, but it hadn't entered my mind that by answering Valerie's cry for help I might be standing in the way of that.

I didn't need this conflict on top of all the others I had taken on already today, but I was damned if I was going to back down on this; I was a professional on a job, not a lovesick teenage bimbo. "It's possible the case will be wrapped in a few days—one way or another—and we could still have some time to spend together. I'm sorry, that's the best I can do right now."

Rob flopped back down in his chair and sighed. "Let's not talk about this right now—let's just go to lunch."

I looked at my watch. "It's not even eleven yet."

"Then we'll make it a long lunch." He stubbed out the cigarette. "Ready to go?"

The reporters were in our faces as soon as we stepped out of the door. "Sergeant Cameron, are there any new developments in the Chandler Stone case?" "Has any new evidence come to light?" "Have any eyewitnesses come forward yet, Sergeant Cameron?"

"I'm really sorry, ladies and gentlemen," Rob said, turning on his world-class charm, "but I have nothing to add to what I've already told you. The Morado Beach Police Department had investigators on the case, and I'm confident we're going to be making an arrest soon." He gave them a boyish smile. "Now if you don't mind . . ."

The Red Sea of recording devices parted, and we walked through the reception area. "I'll be out till about one," Rob told Hogan. "Be sure I get any messages from Pat." Hogan nodded, eyes firmly on the TV.

We stepped out into the bright sunshine that was at least partly responsible for the flood of tourists that the south coast weathers fifty-two weekends a year. "We can take my car," Rob said, and guided me across the lot to a classic Porsche roadster that looked like it had rolled off the line in 1958 and never seen blacktop.

"This is not a car," I said, indicating the spotless white paint job and classic lines. "This is a sex object."

He grinned lasciviously. "Glad you like it."

"I suppose it would be unbearably rude to ask what it cost."

He shrugged. "I got a hell of a deal on it, and anyway, it's my only luxury."

"You mean besides lunches at L'Auberge."

"Today is special. Caley's back in town. Shall we?" He opened the door on my side and closed it after me when I sat down on the glove-soft leather of the seat. He got in the driver's side and we roared out onto the quiet tree-lined street and turned down the hill toward the water.

"What's this gadget?" I asked, pointing to a high-tech black box attached to the dash.

"That's a telephone. Twentieth-century kind of thing. Don't they have those up in the hills?"

"Well, not like this, exactly. We have to hand-crank ours. So Sergeant Yuppie has a car phone?"

"A car like this has to be taken out on a highway and blown out now and then, so if I need to go out of town to see someone on police business, I'll use this car. The phone is for staying in touch with the station."

"I don't suppose you ever snag a citation for 'blowing out' your engine in a fifty-five zone?"

"Well, so far I haven't." He gave me a look of pure innocence. "I guess I've just been lucky."

"I wish *I* were so lucky. So you're driving down the road, and you decide you'd like to eat at Restaurant X, you just call ahead and make reservations without having to stop and find a phone."

"Precisely. Nifty, huh?"

I sat back in the soft leather seat and smiled. "Decadent. Purely decadent."

L'Auberge was a touch of Europe in the midst of all the imitation Mexico that characterized the most touristy areas of Morado Boulevard. Inside it was paneled in rich dark woods, with carved posts and hand-painted ceilings. The waiters were properly snooty and the wine list was properly long and expensive. Rob ordered like a pro and the staff all knew him by name.

We made small talk and reminisced only about the good parts of the good old days. On our way back to the present, we ate our way from an appetizer course of tiny zucchini and carrots done up with dainty strips of chives tied in little bows, and right through to the dessert of fresh raspberries in chocolate baskets accompanied by demitasses of French roast that made my eyes water.

"I'm glad I don't do this every day—I'd look like a house."

"You look awfully good to me, Caley." He stared down at the tablecloth as though hoping to find the right words there. "I've thought about you a lot over the years, you know. A few times I almost had myself convinced to drive up north and find you."

"I wasn't missing."

He took my hand across the table. "I was pretty stupid when I was nineteen. I don't know what I thought I was looking for back then."

"Did you find it?" I remembered how swiftly my life had turned around when Melissa had blown back into town. I removed my hand from his on the pretext of looking for something in my handbag.

"I thought I had for a while. Melissa and I were married for eleven years. Did Valerie ever tell you?"

"Val and I had an understanding never to mention you. By the time it didn't hurt anymore it had become a habit. You said 'were.' What happened?"

"What usually happens, I guess." He paused to light a cigarette. "We never really knew each other, and when things started falling apart and we tried to get acquainted to keep them together, we figured out we were too different to like each other much."

"No children?"

"Nope. You?"

"No." This didn't seem to be the time or place to bring up two stillbirths and four years of on-and-off depression. I pushed a chunk of chocolate around on my dessert plate. "I was married to a newspaper reporter in Cascade until about three years ago. His name is Michael Carlson. He still works up there, and we're pretty good friends as long as we don't see too much of each other." I poured heavy cream into my coffee to trim its claws just a bit. It turned a lighter black.

"Melissa moved down to L.A. and went to work for a movie producer. Ended up marrying him. She's filthy rich."

"How nice for her. I wish I was. So"—I pushed the plate away—"you have to tell me how you ended up on the police force. I always thought you wanted to do anything else."

"So did I, but I guess it was in my blood. I was a sheriff's deputy down in Dago for a while, then when Dad retired from the force, I came back up here, and worked my way up. Once I stopped fighting it, I realized I'd never really wanted to do anything else."

"Where are your parents now? Still in town?"

He shook his head. "They passed away. Mom died shortly after Melissa and I were married, and Dad a few years later."

"I'm sorry, Rob."

He shrugged. "Well, it's been a long time. When my father retired, he started investing his savings and made a pretty good return. When he died, he left me some stocks and securities. A little extra income. That's how I got the Porsche. How about your parents?"

"Oh, they're still around; still pulling up stakes, or maybe never putting any down in the first place. I just opted out of the constant moves after we left here. I'll probably grow old and die right up there in Cascade."

"You could come back down here—they say everyone does, eventually."

"And be an investigator on your turf?" I shook my head. "Somehow I don't think that would work."

"Maybe not. But then maybe you shouldn't be a P.I. in the first place. I always thought you'd do something with your art, like be a famous painter or something."

I shrugged. "Oh, I still draw and paint—I've just given up making a career out of it. Too much chance of failure."

"And there's no failure in investigation?"

"That's different. It's a job. You give it your best and you win some and you lose some. Art is a piece of yourself you put out there for other people to see and evaluate, and if they don't like it, where does that leave you?"

"So if it's just a job, you can tell Valerie you've decided not to take the case."

"I wish I could, Rob. I'm sorry if I've hurt our chances of being able to see each other while I'm here in town, but I can't back out on Val."

"I'm not talking about leaving her in the lurch. You could find her another P.I. San Diego is lousy with them. No offense." He held up his hand as I started to protest. 'Don't make up your mind now—just promise me you'll think about it for a day or two." He flashed that charming smile.

"In a day or two, Tony could be arrested."

Rob leaned forward across the table. The smile was gone. 'Antonio Garza will be arrested whether you take the case or not. Someone shot Chandler Stone through his office window from the street and we're pretty sure it was Garza. Sooner or later we'll place him at the scene—it wasn't that late, and the street couldn't have been that deserted. We really want to nail this one down, Caley. I've had the press down here from L.A. and up from San Diego sniffing around my doorstep playing up the 'unsolved murder' line since Thursday, for God's sake. I've got the sheriff's boys breathing down my neck, wanting in on the action. We're building a case, and when we have the best one we can get, Garza's going to jail. You can't stop that from happening."

I took a chance. "If the case is really that open and shut, maybe you wouldn't mind letting me have a look at the police reports."

He put out the cigarette. "You know I can't do that."

"Yeah. I know. You can't blame me for trying, though, huh?"

"Just take my word for it, it's a dog of a case, okay?"

I shook my head. "You know *I* can't do that." I went for an end run. "I read some newspaper articles about Chandler Stone that Val clipped over the last few days."

"Yeah, this case made papers clear up to San Francisco. Must've been a slow news day."

I shrugged. "Cold-blooded murder sells newspapers. But anyway, besides being savagely handsome and owning half the state, the guy appears to be a shoo-in for Patron Saint of Real Estate Developers. Pardon me, but it all just seems too goddamned wonderful to be true."

"How cliché is that? Who's to say he wasn't a great guy just because everyone says he was a great guy?"

"Well I'm not trying to pick on him now that he's dead and all, but if a very powerful man can make one bitter enemy why not two or three?"

"You're wasting your time, Caley. Tony Garza killed Chandler Stone. He told him he would, and then he did. He's crazier than shit. He threatened Stone's life in front of witnesses."

"That doesn't prove he did it. You'll need more than that if you want to make a case."

"We've got more. Around the corner from Stone's office not a hundred yards from where Garza stood and shot him, a pair of black leather gloves was found in a Dumpster. Garza wears gloves just like them. We ran them through a neutron-activation test, and they were lousy with gunpowder."

I remembered the pair of gloves I had seen at Tony's house. I supposed he had gotten in the habit of wearing them since he was burned.

"So can you get fingerprints from the inside of leather gloves?"

"You know better than that."

"Then what kind of evidence are they against Tony? What you need is some solid physical evidence, or maybe a witness."

Rob's mouth tightened. He signaled the waiter, who brought the check. He paid the tab in cash and we drove back to the station without saying much. Belatedly, I realized I had worn my Mickey Mouse watch throughout the entire nouveau cuisine luncheon that had set Rob back eighty dollars. The thought made me smile.

CHAPTER 5

. . . .

I WAS A COUPLE OF MILES FROM THE STATION AND MOVING inland toward my old neighborhood when I saw the flashing light in the rearview mirror. I glanced at the speedometer. I didn't seem to be going fast enough to warrant attention from the M.B.P.D., but there one was, a charming shade of blue and white, with red lights spinning. I pulled over to the shoulder—still no sidewalks in this part of town, I noted absently—and rolled down my window as I watched a uniformed officer unfold himself from the cruiser and walk up to my door.

I had to crane my neck to look at him. Obligingly, he hunkered down beside my car to give me an easier view. He was at least four inches over six feet, and his hair was a violent shade of strawberry blond under his uniform cap. His face had a permanently sunburned look that made me cringe inside. "Excuse me, ma'am. Are you Ms. Burke?"

"Radar must be getting a lot more sophisticated."

He blushed, if that were possible—it may only have been more sunburn. "No, ma'am. Sergeant Cameron gave me a description of your car. He said to give you this." He pulled a manila envelope from under his arm and handed it to me. "He said you left it at the station by accident."

So Rob had changed his mind; somehow I hadn't expected it. I put the envelope on the passenger seat.

"Fitzpatrick," I said, pointing at his shiny brass nametag. "Your friends call you Fitz?"

"Pat," he replied, ducking his head. It was definitely a blush.

"Yes. Pat. I remember hearing Sergeant Cameron mention you."

"Yes, ma'am. I've been doing some of the investigation work on this big murder case. Legwork, mostly."

"Going for that detective's shield, huh?"

"Well, someday, I hope." He reddened again. There was a shy little boy inside this young man in neatly creased khaki. A few more years of police work might harden him into a real live grown-up, especially if he worked his way up from here to San Diego or L.A. That would be a goddamned shame.

"Well thanks, Pat. You're a credit to the force, and all that. Maybe I'll see you around town again."

He unfolded again. "Yes, ma'am. Very likely. It's a small town."

"Did you grow up here, Pat?"

"Yes, ma'am."

I wanted him to stop calling me that, but I figured it was pretty automatic. He would have been just a kid when I was in high school, I estimated. Funny, although you couldn't pay me to be seventeen again, I didn't really feel any older now than I did then.

"You take it easy," I said, putting the car into gear.

"Yes, ma'am. You, too." He tipped his cap, or seemed to; I couldn't see anything above his elbow.

I pulled off as cautiously as someone who had been pulled over for a moving violation. I'd had a little practice over the years, and it was an ingrained habit.

The envelope, as I'd suspected, contained copies of the police reports. Obviously Rob wasn't as much of a stickler for rules as he had led me to believe. I took them to one of those generic coffee shops by a freeway onramp, took a booth in the back, and spread the stuff out on the table to have a better look.

A waitress approached, coffeepot in hand. She looked over my shoulder at the photographs of the late Chandler Stone's corpse, as found on the blood-soaked carpet of his office, his iron-gray hair taking up blood from a pool that had its origins under a dark chest wound. "I don't guess *he'll* be needing anything," she observed.

I faced down the photographs. "I think I'll just have some coffee."

"Well, I don't blame you, hon," she said, patting me on the shoulder in a motherly way, "your line of work must be awfully tough on the appetite."

The reports were nearly as discouraging as Rob had implied. Chandler Stone had been shot by an unknown assailant with a .38 caliber handgun only three days after several people heard Antonio Garza threaten to kill him. There was one witness to the altercation, Stone's business partner—one Edmund Berenson. He had gotten in on the argument late, and had not heard the subject of the disagreement. Stone had mentioned the incident only in the most general terms once it was past, almost as if it were a big joke.

I got out a small notebook—one of those dime-store spiral jobs that I always own at least a dozen of and can never find the right one when I need it. This one was new and unmarked, so I proceeded to mark it.

I leafed through the reports for the names and addresses of anyone the police had considered important enough to question, and made a note of their alibis.

The handy thing about being interviewed the day after a crime is committed is that you probably remember exactly what you were doing, and with whom. People who are questioned weeks or months after the fact have absolutely no clue as to their whereabouts on a given date at a given time unless they are making it up. All these folks had dandy alibis.

Except, of course, Antonio Garza. Tony's story was that he had been out walking late at night—a habit he had gotten into since his release from the hospital. He had always been known for taking long walks around town, but now he didn't want people to see him. Of course, no one saw him. He said he had walked down from his house where he spent a couple of hours on a rocky beach where he encountered no one, and was never closer than two miles from the murder scene the whole time. But there was no way to prove it.

The police were working very hard to find someone who had seen Tony anywhere near Stone's office at anywhere near the fatal time. They had a ready-made perpetrator in this hotheaded old man who shouted death threats in front of a witness, and they were out to parlay that into an arrest and an easy conviction.

As if that weren't bad enough, several people who knew Tony well had told police he had been a crack pistol shot, at least before the fire, which couldn't hurt matters for a gunman trying to make the shot from across the street, (though it would have been a lucky shot in any case) and his hands, while pretty badly scarred, were not too damaged to hold a gun.

I thought things couldn't get much worse than that, but that's what I got for thinking. Tony had owned a gun of the same type, but had reported it stolen in a burglary two nights after his altercation with Stone. I couldn't have dreamed up a more pat story that stunk worse if I'd tried.

I pushed the papers and photos away. My eyes were burning, my shoulders were tense, and I'd drunk too much coffee. I found myself wishing I could talk to Jake Baronian.

Life turns on the smallest of incidents, sometimes. I had been living in Cascade and been married, not terribly happily, to Michael Carlson, a reporter and feature writer for the local paper. I was drifting then, working a dead-end job much like the last one, my sketchbooks packed away in the bottom of a crate, as they had been for several years. After we gave up trying to have babies, Michael had taken to spending less and less time at home, and I had taken to staring at the wall for hours on end, who knows in which order.

I don't really know what I'd be doing right now if I hadn't run into Jake in the courthouse on the day I went to file for divorce from Michael. Jake was coming out of an elevator with a double armload of overstuffed file folders, and I was going in with two swollen eyes and a handful of damp tissues. A thousand or so sheets of paper went skating out in all directions on the freshly waxed floor, and I looked up to see a fine-looking man about ten or twelve years older than I, with black and silver hair and eyes as sharp and black as obsidian. He was shaking his head sadly.

"Oh, God," I said, "let me help you get this straightened out." I knelt down and started gathering folders and loose papers.

He joined me on the floor. "It's going to take at least a week to straighten all this out. You don't happen to be looking for a job, do you?" I stopped and looked at him, certain he was joking. He wasn't. "I just fired my clerk. She was making twelve-five a year for sitting on her can and watching TV. Can you do clerical?"

"I've never tried," I answered honestly enough as I reached out for an escaped folder.

"That's a shame; you should always try. Here's my card." He reached into a vest pocket and pulled out a dark gray card.

I read it. "Jacob Baronian, Licensed Private Investigator." I studied the man in front of me, trying to decide if he looked like a detective. He didn't. Detectives, I thought, should look boozy and jaded and a little ragged around the edges. This man was neat, clean, a sharp dresser, and gave off an air of humor, intelligence, and education. I decided he didn't even drink. Later, I would find out I was only partly right—Jake was an alcoholic who had been dry for six years.

"I'm Caley Burke, Mr. Baronian, and I *am* sort of looking for a job—a better one, anyway. Do you really hire people who bump into you at the courthouse?"

We shook hands. "I'll admit this is a first. Let's get this mess over to my office and we can at least talk about it."

I went to work the next day as Jake's assistant. A month later he hired someone else to take care of the office work and started training me in the multifarious arts of investigation. It was not always easy, and certainly not always exciting, but I did it well enough, and I never thought about how things might have been if I'd just gone out and found another husband and tried again to have children. Almost never.

Now I was beginning to realize how much I depended on Jake, or at least on the idea of Jake being there to back me up if I needed him. I felt like an astronaut looking down to see the neatly cut end of my tether as I drifted away from everything that was safe in my universe. I decided it was time to give Jake Baronian a call.

"So are you enjoying your vacation, Burke?" he asked. "Surf, sand, sun, and all that?"

I put a finger in my ear to shut out the sounds of the

coffee shop kitchen next to the phone. "I haven't actually made it to any of those attractions yet, Jake. I've gone and taken a case."

"Jesus, I thought you were supposed to be taking it easy! Wasn't this a high school reunion?"

"Yeah, and it was every bit as dreary as I knew it was going to be. But my best friend from school has this problem, or her grandfather has it, actually."

"How bad a problem?"

"Possible murder rap. It looks bad, and I tried to tell them they didn't need a beginner, but . . ."

"You've been doing this for three years, Burke. When are you going to stop calling yourself a beginner?"

"When I stop feeling like one, I guess."

"Didn't I teach you everything you know?"

"Yeah, you did. Why didn't you teach me everything *you* know, instead?"

"All in good time, my dear. So what is it you're calling to hear me say to you?"

"I don't know, Jake. That I don't have to take the case, that you'll come running down here and make everything all right, that there's still a Santa Claus—I don't know."

"You don't have to take the case."

"I know that. But on the other hand I do, you know what I mean?"

"I can't come down and take over for you."

"Shit."

"I really can't get away, and I'm not sure I should if I could. This seems like the perfect opportunity for you to prove to yourself that you've got what it takes to handle a big one on your own. You certainly don't have to prove it to me at this point. I have confidence in you; now it's time for you to develop some in yourself."

"But it's such a big, bad, ugly case, Jake. It's not just another whiplash faker, it's murder. First degree."

"The techniques are the same whether you're playing chopsticks or a Mozart serenade. You start by sitting down and putting your fingers on the keys." Jake had taken up the piano a couple of months previously, and it showed in his most recent metaphors.

"My fingers are shaking."

"By the time you play eight bars, they won't be. Trust me on this one, Burke. If you give this case all you've got and you still feel like you're in over your head, call me back and I'll give you the number of a guy in San Diego."

"Okay. I'll try. By the way, have I ever won an argument with you?"

"Not that I can recall. Now wrap it up and get down on the beach for a few days."

"The sun and I don't get along."

"So wear a hat. You've been working too hard, and now you've gone and got yourself more work. When this vacation is over, you're going to need a vacation."

I hung up before I realized we hadn't settled the Santa Claus question.

I returned to my booth and the police reports, not terribly encouraged, but knowing that at least Jake thought I had what it took. It would be up to me not to make a liar out of him. I wrote down the address and phone number of Stone's office downtown. Time for the investigator to investigate.

CHAPTER 6

"GOOD AFTERNOON, STONE AND BERENSON." THE VOICE sounded familiar, but so were a lot of things today.

"Good afternoon. I'm calling from California Central Life and Casualty. Do you mind if I ask you about the forms of coverage you currently carry?" I flavored my lie with a very slight Southern accent, such as one might retain after living half a lifetime in California.

There was a brief pause, then the voice returned, somewhat puzzled. "I suppose that would be all right, but we're really not interested in acquiring any additional insurance."

"I understand perfectly. I just need to ask you a few quick questions." I consulted a list I had jotted down and went through the questionnaire as might the ex–Southern belle I was constructing for the occasion.

I had always been too shy to go out for drama in high school, but I dearly loved the minor histrionics I could sometimes get away with in the detective business. This instinctive chameleon trick was one of the things Jake loved about me. "Thank you so much for your cooperation, Miss . . . ?"

"Kramer. Crystal Kramer."

Another ghost from the past. "Thank you, Miss Kramer," I said, and "Bingo," when I had hung up the phone and made a large left-handed checkmark next to the words "Business Partners—Mutual Beneficiaries?" I wasn't any more interested in Crystal Kramer than I had been in 1975, but I decided it was time to make the acquaintance of Mr. Berenson of Stone and Berenson, Inc.

My memory of specifics was pretty foggy where Morado Beach was concerned, which is why I hadn't realized that the address where Chandler Stone bought and sold huge chunks of California was right across the street from the Hayden-Morris Gallery, Val Hayden's business.

Whoever killed Stone, according to the diagrams in the police report, must have been standing just outside the gallery. It was after nine, and the sidewalks still rolled up at six in this part of town, leaving the night life to Morado Boulevard. The street would have been practically deserted.

A janitor in another building had heard a shot and saw someone running down the street, but from upstairs and almost a block away, he could give no specifics. He thought it was a man, but admitted he could be wrong. So far, the police had found no one else who had been close enough to hear anything out of the ordinary or remembered seeing anyone outside on the street around that time.

Busy bees had repaired the window, and there was no sign from downstairs that anything unusual had taken place. A fancy Mexican restaurant with an Aztec-style name I couldn't pronounce occupied the corner of the building directly under Stone's office, which was reached by a tile and terra-cotta stairway with a wrought-iron railing and several potted plants. Somebody around here was doing a land-office business in palm trees.

I climbed the steps to a plush reception area with a huge brass signature on the wall reading "Stone" and another reading "Berenson."

The receptionist glanced up as soon as I got within her territory. Crystal Kramer hadn't changed much since high school. She looked and dressed much the same then—pastels and high heels and frilly collars—and she curled her mousy hair with rollers. She probably looked thirty or so from the day she was born.

"I'd like to see Mr. Berenson," I told her.

"Do you have an appointment?" I could tell by her tone she knew damned well I didn't and wanted me to know it.

Stretching the truth was out with Miss Kramer. Maybe the truth would prove effective.

"My name is Caley Burke and I'm a private investigator. I need to speak with him about Chandler Stone." That was unspecific as hell, but very official-sounding, which was pretty much what I was after.

Her mouth fell open just a bit. For a moment I couldn't tell if she was reacting to my name or Chandler Stone's, but then she smiled the sickly smile I remembered so well. "Caley Burke? Is that really you? Well, I guess I should have recognized you right away."

I couldn't see any reason why she should. Crystal and I were never what you could call friends, or even good acquaintances. I was nice to her in those days, in a distant sort of way, but always kept her at arm's length for fear she would latch on to me in her desperation to have people like her. We had gone out for hamburgers and a movie a couple of times, but we didn't even have enough in common to get us through one real conversation without awkwardness.

Crystal had, I recalled from her interview with the police, been playing cards with her parents when Chandler Stone had been shot. Hearts, I believe.

"Yes, it's me, all right." I slipped right into cliché mode just standing this close to her; sometimes being a chameleon isn't all it's cracked up to be. "I don't think I saw you at the reunion last night."

"Oh, I had to miss it. I really wanted to be there, but I had to go out of town on business, and by the time I got back . . . what was it you wanted to see Mr. Berenson about?"

Lie? Truth? I weighed my options. "I'm investigating the death of Chandler Stone."

Crystal's eyes widened. "Oh. Are you with the police?"

"Not exactly. Can you check and see if he'll talk with me?" I tried to look and sound like any old high school buddy might, asking a tiny favor.

"Of course. I'm sorry, Caley. I'll see if Mr. Berenson will see you. Please, have a seat."

She talked into her phone and within ten seconds Mr. Berenson appeared in the doorway.

There are handsome men and then there are *handsome* men. Edmund Berenson probably snapped enough heads around on enough necks to get kickbacks from all the local chiropractors. His eyes were a pale blue and he had a slightly tanned and exquisitely mustached face under a perfect head of black wavy hair, with just a hint of gray beginning at the temples.

Beneath the casually dressy clothes there was a suggestion of muscle, neither too much nor too little. Parts of my brain that don't think things out were impressed in spite of the other parts' caution. His movements were careful and calculated after the fashion of men who know they are being watched wherever they go. Berenson's alibi involved an exercise bunny from his health club. Not remotely surprising.

"Ms. Burke. Won't you step into my office." I did, and he kept talking as he sat behind his desk and gestured me to a seat opposite. "It's a terrible tragedy, what happened to Chandler— we're still in a state of shock around here."

The state of shock at Stone & Berenson looked a lot to me like a state of business as usual, but the kind of money these people dealt in made long periods of mourning impractical and unlikely.

"How can I help you, Ms. Burke?" he inquired. His deep voice was controlled, almost schooled. A real pro, this one.

"I've been hired to look into the facts surrounding Mr. Stone's death."

"May I ask whom you're working for?"

"Of course. I'm working for the family of Antonio Garza. The police are cooperating with me, and of course I'll let them in on any details I uncover in the course of my investigation."

I sat up straight in my chair and folded my hands in my lap, trying on a bit of demure and nonthreatening for Mr. Berenson. Meanwhile I looked around. "The police have been very helpful, but my investigation is necessarily separate from theirs, and I will have to speak with everyone who was close to Mr. Stone. I realize you've already spoken with the investigating officer, Detective Sergeant Cameron."

"Well, yes, but of course I'll want to cooperate any way I can." I tried reading the face behind that statement, but it was closed off behind a perfect mask of sincerity. Or what the hell, maybe he really was sincere. Who was I to say?

"Thank you." I flashed him a smile. "You must have known Mr. Stone almost as well as anyone. Can you think of anyone who might have, well, wanted him dead?"

"Chandler was one of the most beloved men in Morado Beach," Berenson intoned, tenting his fingers in the manner of one who wants to impart weight to his words. "He was on several civic committees, including the board of the North County Children's Hospital. He was unfailingly generous with his time and money for any worthy cause; he was almost single-handedly responsible for saving the old Seaside Hotel, one of the oldest buildings on this part of the coast, when it was slated for demolition."

I wondered if Berenson were rehearsing for the eulogy at the funeral tomorrow. Chandler Stone's sainthood had another champion.

"Yes, everything I've heard so far about Mr. Stone suggests that he was a very popular man. Still, someone did shoot him. Could it have been a case of mistaken identity, perhaps?"

"There was one person sick enough to murder a man like Chandler." The ice-blue eyes narrowed. I waited.

"Your client, Antonio Garza."

"Please tell me why you think that. Regardless of what you may think, I really am in the business of serving justice."

"Because I heard him threaten to do it."

"Go on, please." This wasn't news of course, but attitudes, postures, and tones of voice don't translate well into print. It's always better to face someone and get it through all senses.

"Chandler and I were out to dinner, about three nights before . . ." His hands made a gesture suggesting a loss for words. "We ate at La Romana, down on the beach. We left the restaurant rather late; they were closing the place, actually. Garza accosted Chandler in the parking lot on the way to the car while I was still inside. When I came out, I heard him shouting at Chandler, accusing him of seducing some woman. He didn't mention a name, just kept saying Stone had done it to get back at him, and he'd pay for it. That kind of thing over and over."

"Did he say anything more specific? Did he actually threaten his life?"

"He said, 'Your life is worth nothing. *You* are worth nothing. I'll kill you like I'd kill a bug.' "

"What did Mr. Stone say back to him?"

"Hardly anything. He actually seemed amused. It shows how cool Chandler was—how self-possessed. He could look at that monster without flinching. I could hardly look at him at all. That was the only time I'd seen Garza since he was released from the hospital. It shook me."

I couldn't be entirely unsympathetic with Berenson's reaction to Tony, but I had to wonder what had amused Chandler Stone about having his life threatened.

"Would it be possible for me to see Mr. Stone's office?"

"Of course, but you understand the carpet has been replaced and the walls repainted since . . ."

"Yes. I just wanted to have a look. Would it be all right if I used your rest room first?"

"Certainly. It's across the hall." He opened his center drawer and removed a key, which he pocketed.

I killed most of a minute in the rest room, then opened the door a tiny crack and peeked out. Berenson's chair was empty—he had probably gone to unlock Stone's office—and Crystal was turned toward a computer monitor and away from me. I pushed the door open very slowly and tiptoed back across the hall to Berenson's office.

I'm not sure what I was looking for; maybe I just thought I'd get lucky in the few seconds I was allotting myself to look the room over. I slid open the top drawer of the desk. The interior was as sterile and lacking normal human office clutter as if he had only rented the office for the day as a front. I closed it again, and granting myself a few more seconds against my better judgment, I peeked into the trash container.

I lifted the oak veneer basket and tilted it to one side, shaking the contents a bit to shuffle them. There was the usual jumble of pinfeed paper edges—whoever discovers a use for that stuff is going to make millions—some wadded up sheets of paper that I dared not unwad for fear of being heard, and at the very bottom the thing I would have been looking for if I'd had any idea what I was looking for in the first place.

The Daily Racing Form is a fairly common sight on this part of the coast, with Del Mar only a pleasant, eucalyptus-sheltered drive away. You can buy one at the track, or in any liquor store or grocery market. Edmund Berenson had a subscription, with neat little computer labels made out to his home address. Hard core, Ed.

I heard steps on the carpet and set the basket down, taking a step away from the desk.

"Lose something, Ms. Burke?"

"I thought I left my sunglasses in here. Guess they must be in the car." I managed a smile, hoping my face wasn't as white as it felt, and walked past him through the door.

Berenson escorted me across the foyer to a set of double oak doors that were a perfect match with all the stucco and tile. He opened them and followed me in.

Except for the smell of paint and carpet glue, the office might have been waiting for Chandler Stone to return from a long lunch. A huge oak desk dominated the center of the room, sunk into thick pile carpet. A row of windows over-looked California Street and directly across the street was the Hayden-Morris Gallery.

It was a glorious Saturday in tourist season, and families in bright new clothes wandered in and out of the gallery and other establishments, looking to spend their traveler's checks on expensive souvenirs of their vacations.

"He would have had to be standing right in front of the gallery over there," Berenson said. "That's what the police determined by the angle of the bullet. Probably a pretty fair shot, too. A pistol doesn't have all that much accuracy from that distance. Then there's the refraction from the window to consider . . ."

"Are you familiar with firearms, Mr. Berenson?"

"I keep a gun in my house, but I haven't done much shooting since I was a boy." The police reports had mentioned Berenson's gun—the same caliber as the murder weapon. He had consented to having it tested, and it did not match up with the fatal slug.

"Thank you for your cooperation, Mr. Berenson. It's possible I may need to speak with you again. Would that be all right?"

"Just call ahead next time, Miss Burke." He smiled a businesslike smile and shook my hand.

From the pay phone downstairs, I called ahead to Barbara Stone, Chandler Stone's widow, but her maid told me she was under sedation by her doctor's orders. On the fatal night, while Stone was working late and waiting to die, Barbara and the maid, Elena Sanchez, had been home together. Elena had spent the evening in her apartment over the garage, watching TV. Barbara had been reading in the living room. Not a classic seamless alibi, but not bad, either. I left a message saying I would call again tomorrow, and walked over to the gallery.

I looked in, but Val was busy with a group of white-haired ladies in pastel knit shorts, and I saw David waiting for her. After this morning's unpleasantness, I really didn't feel like facing him.

Her assistant had gone out of town on a family emergency, Val'd told me that morning, and it didn't look like she'd have much free time anyway until she got back. I decided to pick up some industrial strength sunscreen and go to the beach.

CHAPTER 7

EXCEPT FOR A BIG CHUNK OF COASTLINE THAT'S OWNED BY the U.S. government and houses a marine base, the entire length of California Highway 101 between Los Angeles and San Diego is a mass of beach towns that have grown into one another over the years to form an unbroken strip of expensive rentals, convenience stores, and T-shirt shops.

Fifty years ago many of these towns had started off as artists' colonies. Galleries followed, then expensive boutiques. Any weekend day would find the winding seaside avenues crowded with thousands of strollers, shoppers, and cruisers out for what they were out for.

Most of these towns seemed born to be what they had become, as though the outcome were inevitable, even desirable. Morado Beach, on the other hand, had the air of having become a tourist center by virtue of geography. It never had the heart for glamour, but like a girl who discovers that all she has to do to get a date every Saturday night is to put out for everybody, it put on its makeup and flashed a smile for the folks on their way down south from Los Angeles or up north from San Diego.

The big selling point, as with all these towns, was the Pacific Ocean. If you've lived by it all your life, maybe it's just a bunch of water, but to people who have come a thousand miles to wait in line at Disneyland and go home

46

with a TV star's autograph and a second-degree sunburn, it's a goddamned bloody marvel. To the surfers, it's a way of life.

I parked my car above the state beach in the one spot I could see for miles, only just vacated by a nice-looking family in Sea World baseball caps. After covering all my exposed parts with factor 44, I crossed the highway and headed down the sand-worn beach stairs.

The water was still a little cold for most swimmers, but south coast surfers don't wait for warm water. The waves were dotted with bright wetsuits and vivid boards and sun-bleached heads turned toward the sea.

I sat in the sand and watched them paddling out by twos and threes, catching the waves and riding them in, over and over in a rhythm as natural as the sea. Now and again a surfer would wipe out, his board flying up to the end of its tether and jerking back down into the water. When the wave passed, he would be back aboard waiting for the next good one.

One surfer rode his wave in to the sand and untethered his board. His hair was a mass of blond spikes on top, trailing down to his shoulders on the sides. He walked up toward and almost past me before he stopped and stared. "Caley? Is that you?"

I looked up into a pair of bright blue eyes in a rugged young face that seemed very familiar somehow.

"Andy? Andy McCain?"

"None other. I'll be goddamned—Caley Burke. I haven't seen you since I was nine or ten years old."

"Well I don't think you've had much need for a baby-sitter recently." Andy would be about twenty-five now. I was only about seven years older, but seeing him a foot and a half taller and unquestionably grown up made me feel like his grandmother. It was the same face I remembered—a face more interesting than handsome, like his father's, with his mother's blond coloring.

"Nope, not lately."

He smiled a crooked smile I remembered well from when he used to use it on me to get whatever he wanted, back when he was nine years old and I was his baby-sitter. He set the board down and plopped down in the sand beside me. "So what brings you back to town? Are you here for good?"

"For good or ill, only for a week. Six days, now. How's your mom?"

"Not too good, right now; some doer of good deeds shot her husband four days ago." His left hand pulled at a bracelet he wore; a piece of wetsuit tied around his wrist.

"Shot . . . you mean Barbara Stone is . . ."

"The former Barbara McCain."

"I had no idea. I was planning on stopping by to see her tomorrow."

"She's not in the old house anymore. She gave it to me a few months after she moved into Stone's place in Costa Azul. She's been married to Stone for about six years, now. By some strange coincidence, that's almost exactly the same amount of time I've been gone from home." His smile was humorless now. "Chandler Stone was not my favorite person. I can't even speak well of him now that he's dead." The bracelet snapped. Andy cursed and rubbed at the welt it raised on the inside of his wrist.

"Some people around town seem to think he was some kind of holy man."

"Yeah, well, most people who didn't know him really liked him." He looked up. "I've gotta get out of this suit. Come on up to the van with me, okay?"

I brushed the sand off my backside and followed him up the beach stairs to the parking lot, where he opened the doors of a battered blue kombi whose side windows were entirely covered in stickers advertising various brands of surf gear. After stowing the board inside, he unzipped the wetsuit and peeled it off, stepping out in faded pink shorts and slipping into a white T-shirt that showed a mushroom cloud overshadowing a group of surfers out beyond the breakers. Day-Glo pink and orange letters proclaimed "Hot Surf."

"Would you like a Coke?" Andy offered. "Greasy taco? I'm on my way to Chihuahuaburger. I'll even buy."

Chihuahuaburger was the local nickname for the Little Mexico taco stand a mile or so up Morado Boulevard from the state beach. It had been a favorite chowdown spot when I was in high school, mostly because of the greasy fifty-cent tacos that were addictive beyond all reason. The tacos were eighty-nine cents now, and every bit as greasy as ever. I ordered two and took a handful of napkins as my first line of defense.

We walked away from the service window and over to a picnic table by the side of the highway. It was laboring under several additional coats of paint since I had sat there last, but I still recognized some of the names carved into the top.

Andy set down his tacos and straddled a bench. "So what are you doing these days? You trade in baby-sitting for a bunch of your own rug rats?"

I shook my head. "No. No rug rats. Maybe knowing you cured me. I'm a private investigator."

"No shit? What a trip. You carry a gun around and shoot it out with the bad guys like Magnum?"

I was carrying a gun, but habit and Jake's training kept me from mentioning it. "If nobody thinks you're armed," Jake was fond of saying, "nobody will take you seriously as a threat. That's exactly what you want."

I shrugged. "Mostly I shoot it out with paperwork. The job's not as exciting as it's cracked up to be. What have you been doing since you grew up on me while my back was turned?"

He pointed to his shirt. "That's me. Hot Surf. Best surf shop from Dago to Onofre."

I shook my head. "I always thought you'd grow up to be a lawyer."

Andy grinned. "So did Dad. It's still not something we talk about a whole lot, but I think he's beginning to understand."

"Does your dad still practice here in town?"

"Yep. Right up on California Street, across from the late Chandler Stone's offices." He took a bite of his taco and chewed thoughtfully. "I don't think he shot him, though."

I had to agree it was a pretty ludicrous thought that mild-mannered Brian McCain would stand across the street and fire a bullet into another human being. It was never safe to assume anything in this business, though; people do some pretty uncharacteristic things when pushed, and Brian's wife had somehow ended up married to Stone. That sort of thing has been known to piss people off.

"I think I ought to be straight with you, Andy. I'm investigating Stone's death for the family of a suspect in the murder."

"Tony Garza?"

"What made you say that?"

"It's the name on everyone's lips when the subject comes up. He and Stone had some kind of feud going ever since he got out of the hospital."

"Well, you're right—that's who I'm working for. Valerie and David think their grandfather is innocent and they want to keep him out of jail. I'm trying to interview everyone the police have spoken to—I assume that includes you and your dad."

"Yep. You can ask me anything. Dad's another matter, though. He left town this morning to go stay with my grandma. She's eighty-something years old and feeling poorly, as they say."

According to the police report, Brian McCain had been having dinner with his legal assistant, who was also his lover. He spent the night at her place. Andy, a chip off the old block, was likewise covered by an all-night visit to a young woman who worked at the bar next door to his place of business. It all seemed fine for now. Poking holes in alibis was not difficult, should it ever be needed, but that was not on my list of things to do today.

"Well, I'm not going to grill you over tacos and sodas. Maybe we can make an appointment to get together tomorrow or something. There is something I'm curious about, though."

"Shoot."

"The feud between Tony and Stone. I know you hadn't exactly been seeing a lot of your stepfather lately, but do you know what it might have been about?"

"Not really. Well"—he took a sip of his drink—"it might have had something to do with Stone finding out that Tony and my mother had been sleeping together on and off for the past twenty years."

CHAPTER 8

. . . .

TONY AND BARBARA STONE. THAT EXPLAINED THE FEUD, BUT it didn't explain what Berenson had said. He had heard Tony accuse Stone of seducing some woman "to get back at me." Now I knew what he felt Stone had been getting back for, but I still didn't have a clue as to who the mysterious woman was.

Tony had had a lot of mistresses over the years, and was sentimental about all of them. All Stone would have had to do to piss him off would be to break one of their hearts. To hear Andy tell it, he was capable of that and almost anything else you cared to name, up to and including the mutilation of small animals.

I told Andy I would come by and see "Hot Surf" tomorrow, and had him take me back to my car. It was only midafternoon, but I was ready to call it a day.

I turned inland a block and drove past Tony's house on my way back to Irene's from the state beach. The screen door stood open and David's car was nowhere in sight, but I couldn't bring myself to stop. I wanted to talk to Tony, needed to talk to him, but not without the buffer of Val and David. Something inside me recoiled at the thought of facing him alone, and I was deeply ashamed of it.

When I got to Irene's I indulged myself in another shower and a nap. It was only my first day on the case, but I was totally exhausted. Seeing Tony, reacting as I did inside to the

51

horror that the disfigured arouse in us, had colored the rest of the day for me.

Two years ago, in Cascade, Jake had a client whose face had been severely burned in a fire. I did a lot of the work on her case, and we had several occasions to talk. I remember how seeing her, knowing she had once looked normal, perhaps even pretty, made me wonder how she faced people, seeing their reactions in their eyes, and held her head high.

If it were me, I wondered, who was turned into an object of horror, would I end my life? Probably not. Would I ever be able to leave my house and go out in public? Probably not. One thing for certain, I decided—if it were me, I would never again have a mirror in my house.

There were no mirrors in Antonio Garza's house. There was only David's portrait of a handsome man with hair like a silver lion's mane and dancing brown eyes—the man a dozen women in Morado Beach had been secretly or otherwise in love with; the man who had made lemonade for Valerie and me on the patio of his little house, and talked with us while he painted a world of pueblos and canyons neither of us had ever seen.

Valerie had had to sneak out in those days to see Tony, since her mother would not allow them contact. David defied his mother and saw his grandfather openly, but Irene hated him for it, I think. Hate came easily to Irene.

Valerie was less inclined to make waves, and used me as her cover. We would drive from the big Spanish mansion on the beach, in the opposite direction, in case Irene should be looking, then drive inland a block and double back to the little blue house where we would spend the afternoon watching Tony paint.

Later, when I had more confidence in myself, I brought him my sketches. He commented on them, praising me when I earned it, always showing me where I could improve without negating the worth of what I had done. It was because of him and David that I had kept drawing and painting.

I closed my eyes and tried to bring that Tony back, but I could not remember what he looked like then, because what he looked like now was burned into my eyes. I fell asleep with that image before me.

I woke to the sound of a key in the front door lock. It was pitch-black in the bedroom. "Val? Is that you?"

Some lights came on downstairs. There was a rustle of bags and parcels being set down, and keys coming out of the lock. I threw off the coverlet I'd pulled up over myself in my sleep and padded downstairs barefoot. A huge pile of shopping bags and boxes lay in the middle of the entryway, topped by a pair of delicate Italian-made shoes. The living room was dark, but a light was on in the kitchen.

"Hello," I ventured, walking toward the light.

A figure appeared in the doorway, featureless in silhouette. It reached around and flipped on the room light. It was Irene Hayden.

"Caley!" she said. "Valerie said you'd be here this week. Come in and talk with me while I make some coffee." She turned back into the kitchen and I followed.

I wasn't sure how to bring up the fact that I hadn't been expecting her to come home until after I had gone back up north; it was probably better to let it pass. As for my connection to Tony's problem, I would definitely not be the first to bring it up. Irene's reaction to any mention of Tony was usually to ignore the comment and change the subject; she had become eerily good at it over the years, so that watching her go into that mode, you almost got the idea that she had not heard, or that the words "Tony" and "father" had no meaning in her universe. It was one subject about which she was definitely not rational.

Having a Mexican father had been a constant blight on Irene's growing up in Morado Beach, Val and David had told me years ago. She had her mother's fair skin, and bleached her dark hair blond from high school on, but the name Garza hung on her like a dirty garment, keeping her out of the crowd of spoiled rich Anglo kids she so desperately wanted to join.

She set her sights on Peter Hayden because he was older, out of college, and established in his own small engineering company. He wasn't looking for a wife, but he was flattered when a clearly beautiful girl threw herself at him. He married her when she told him she was pregnant, because he was incapable of doing anything else.

Eventually, Peter made her a rich woman, and she was content to live graciously, spend money, and feel protected from her parentage by his Anglo name. Morado Beach was not such a high-society place that they could afford to ignore Irene once she had Peter's money and success behind her, and so finally she became the social butterfly she so desperately wanted to be.

Over the years Irene and Peter had come to an arrangement that suited them both: Peter spent at least six months of every year abroad, and so did Irene—but not the same six months. While he was in China or Africa building bridges, she reigned over the beach house. Soon after he came home to see to his local interests, she would be off on an extended trip somewhere.

The only blight on her contentedness was the fact that Peter refused to move from his hometown, and she must eventually come home to the fact that everyone in town knew who her father was—a Mexican, a womanizer, and a drunk. She coped with this by ignoring it, and him, but her hate was as solid as her father was nonexistent. I wasn't the only person who found it a little frightening.

I watched Irene go through the familiar actions of brewing coffee. She made small talk about her trip out of town, about shopping, about the traffic and the tourists. It all seemed unnaturally bright, almost brittle. I decided to feel for cracks, despite my better judgment.

"It's a tragedy about Chandler Stone, isn't it? Valerie showed me all the newspaper clippings. I mean the guy seems to have been the best thing to happen to this town in years—saving the Seaside, all those new developments, creating all those new jobs—and then somebody shoots him. It's really hard to figure, isn't it?"

Irene had stopped dead when I started talking, but by the time she turned around, her face was perfectly composed.

"Yes, it is difficult to understand how someone who's done so much good for the community could possibly have an enemy."

Her eyes were focused somewhere just above and behind me, and it was all I could do not to turn around and see if someone was standing there. What really got to me, though, was the difference between her words and her eyes. Her voice, schooled to bland perfection, was in control, but her eyes were like stones.

She turned back around and got two cups and two saucers out of the cupboard. "Let's take some coffee and sit in the front room, shall we?"

I forced a smile as she handed me a cup, and followed her into the living room. The sun had sunk beneath the darkened ocean, and only a faint orange glow lit the seaward side of the room. Irene set her cup down on a polished mahogany table and drew the drapes on the three tall windows that faced the beach, a job normally performed by her housekeeper around this time of day, but Amelia was on a trip to Mexico to visit with her family.

I watched Irene turning on lamps around the room and wondered about her reaction to my question about Stone. Had she hated Stone, too? Or was it something else entirely?

I was a guest in Irene's house, and I was investigating a murder in order to help someone I knew for certain she hated. Irene hadn't been questioned by the police, having had no obvious connection with Stone, but Val had mentioned that at the time of the murder Irene had been shopping in Balboa Beach and had stayed overnight. Was there a graceful way, I wondered, to find out where? Did I have the guts to dig deeper in these circumstances? And would I keep digging if things got less than graceful?

I was still making up my mind, cup in hand, when the front door opened and Val and Russ walked in with the kids, saving me from embarrassment or intimidation, whichever.

Val was as surprised to see Irene as I had been. "Mom! I thought you were going to be in L.A. the rest of the week." She crossed the room to her mother, who turned her cheek for a brief kiss, the most affection I had ever seen her allow anyone to show her.

Irene nodded to Russ, who nodded back. Russ and I shook hands. It was startling to me every time I saw Russ Morris how much he resembled Peter Hayden. Val never got much in the way of a normal relationship from her father, and she appeared to have gone out of her way to find him in her husband. Like Peter, Russ was tall, thin, and blond, a one-color man whose face disappeared when he took off his glasses. Also like Peter, Russ's work consumed the majority of his time, though his accounting business kept him a lot closer to home than Peter Hayden's did.

I was reintroduced to Patrick and Kate, now twelve and eight, who hadn't seen me for quite a few years. They reminded me of little clones of Russ—long-faced, serious, and in training to be a bit dull—but with Valerie's dominant hair and eye coloring to liven their looks up a bit. As soon as possible, they excused themselves politely, then headed upstairs to the television, arguing about which program they were going to watch.

Russ went to the liquor cabinet and poured himself a shot of Scotch. "Enjoying your visit so far?" he inquired. I wondered if Val hadn't told him about my involvement in Tony's problem, or if he was doing what everyone did around Irene—tiptoeing around any mention of Tony.

"Well, I've managed to hit a couple of high spots today. I've been to L'Auberge and Little Mexico."

Val came over and put an arm around my shoulder. "That must mean you're ready for some real food. Let's all go to Garcia's."

The thought of a giant chile relleno drowning in salsa made me realize how hungry I was. "Garcia's sounds wonderful." I looked down at my wrinkled dress. A change of clothes was definitely in order, my third today. I was beginning to get dizzy. Back up in Cascade, I usually spent my off hours in ancient jeans and large T-shirts, curled up with a book, going to the movies, or sketching down by the river. "Give me five minutes to change."

"I ate on the way down," said Irene. "I couldn't possibly." I also knew that she wouldn't be caught dead in Garcia's, so the invitation had obviously been meant to exclude her anyway. Val turned to Russ. "How about you? Garcia's sound good?"

"Well, we did have that late lunch, hon. And I don't think I'm in the mood for Mexican, anyway." He smiled apologetically.

"Then let's eat someplace else. You name it."

"No, why don't you and Caley go alone and catch up on gossip without me? The kids and I will get something out of the freezer."

"Are you sure, Russ? We could go for pasta instead."

"No, go on. Have a good time." He kissed her cheek, and I was reminded of the earlier contact between Val and Irene.

"I guess it's settled," Val said to me. "Go ahead and change. We'll take my car."

I went upstairs to my room, glad that Val and I would be eating alone. Russ and I had absolutely nothing in common, to the point where we sometimes found conversation difficult. The first few times Val and I had arranged to meet during one of their art buying trips, we had tried socializing together, but had abandoned the attempts years before.

Nowadays Val went on those trips alone anyway, and Russ's contribution to the Hayden-Morris Gallery was to keep the finances in order. He neither knew nor cared about art, but enjoyed seeing Val's success. The kids were more like their father, and would probably grow up to be junior accountants in his business, but Val was devoted to all of them anyway.

"I don't want you to think I'm pressuring you, but has anything turned up?" We had finished our chiles rellenos during a conversation about the old days in Morado Beach, and how much the place had changed since I'd been gone. Now we were on our second round of Dos Equis. I couldn't speak for Val, but I was feeling pretty mellow.

"A couple of things." I opened my handbag and took out my notebook. "I talked with Stone's partner, Edmund Berenson. He confirmed the story about Tony's argument with Stone. Tomorrow I plan to do some asking around the neighborhood of La Romana to find out if anyone might have possibly heard any of the argument between Tony and Stone. I'm also going to do some checking on Edmund Berenson. I don't know what you think, but he seems awfully showbiz for a real estate developer."

Val nodded. "Yeah, I'd have to agree with that. I know *I* never liked him."

"He's also the beneficiary of a largish insurance policy on Stone's life."

"Christ!"

"Well, don't jump to any conclusions. He and Stone had each other insured for business purposes. It's not really all that uncommon, but it might be a good idea to find out if he's been around—ever made any news—that sort of thing. For that matter, it wouldn't hurt to check on both of them."

"Both of who?"

"Both Berenson and Stone, dummy." I laughed. "Have another beer." I signaled the waitress for two more and decided to sleep in just a bit tomorrow.

"I don't understand. Why would you need to check on Stone?"

"Valerie, thinking well of the dead is of absolutely no practical use in my line of business. Being a murder victim doesn't qualify one for sainthood, and frankly, people who die violently have very frequently done things to make that kind of demise a likelihood."

She pondered this for a moment, biting her lip. "All right. Is there anything else?"

"Well, yes. Did you know your grandfather was having an affair with Barbara Stone?"

Valerie's eyes widened. "I knew they had a thing going when she was married to Brian McCain, but I assumed when she married Chandler it was over. It wasn't?"

"Not according to Andy McCain. Did Tony tell you what the argument with Stone was about?"

She shook her head. "He said it was a matter of honor. He refused to discuss it with me."

"Yeah, he's good at that. Well, Berenson overheard part of it—it was about some woman. Not Barbara—someone else."

The waitress picked that moment to arrive with the beers and pour them into our glasses. When she left I looked at Valerie again. She was sitting very still, staring into space as though she were trying to piece together something important.

"Hey, Val, come back. Earth to Valerie." I reached out and touched her. She looked through me for a moment. I remembered Irene's earlier reaction to the mention of Stone's name. So maybe it hadn't been hate. Wonderful. "Is it Irene? She acted absolutely eerie when I mentioned Stone this evening. Do you think she could have been sleeping with Stone? Do you think Tony would have killed him for that?"

Val picked up her purse. "I have to get out of here. Can you drive?"

"Sure. Go get in the car. I'll take care of this and be right out."

Val fled, and I paid the check and left a tip beside my untouched beer. She handed me the keys as I got into the driver's seat, and we pulled off heading west. Half a mile from the beach, I pulled over to let her throw up.

CHAPTER 9

· · · · · · · · · · · · · · ·

I CALLED MICHAEL AT HOME FIRST THING IN THE MORNING. He wasn't awake yet. "Caley, it's Sunday. On Sundays I sleep late. How quickly you forget."

"We haven't lived together for three years, Michael, but I'm sorry anyway. I need a favor."

"Favor. Let's see, now—where are we on favors?" He whistled tunelessly as he pretended to look up the score. "Oh, well, it looks like we're three for two so far this year. That's one you still owe me, you understand."

"Perfectly. Okay, you now own my soul. And I promise to lie prettily to the next girlfriend you introduce me to. I can make you look like a hell of a catch if you make sure her I.Q. is in two figures."

"Deal. What can I do for you?"

"There's a real estate developer down here by the name of Edmund Berenson. He was partners with a guy named Chandler Stone until last Wednesday night. That's when Stone was shot by an unknown assailant. The funeral's this afternoon."

"Holy shit." His voice became instantly alert; nothing a reporter likes like a good story. "So what do you need to know?"

"I'd be interested to find out whether either of them has ever been worth any ink from about seven years ago on back.

Stone came here from Los Angeles—Berenson may have, too. You might want to start there."

"I think I have a couple of friends in L.A. who might be able to get ahold of that kind of thing. I didn't know you'd gone down south to do a murder investigation."

"It came as a surprise to me, too." I gave him Irene's number and he told me he'd get back to me later in the day.

I called the police department, but Rob was out of reach. I left a message saying I would check back this afternoon. We hadn't parted on the best of terms yesterday, and I figured it was time to mend some fences. Meanwhile, I had a date with the races.

The racetrack at Del Mar is one of several major attractions along the south coast that keep every hotel and motel between Tijuana and Orange County filled to capacity every weekend night for four or five months of the year. Like any gambling enterprise, it is frequented by a combination of tourists, amateurs, and pros.

The tourists come for the experience, lose a few bucks and go home. The amateurs play hunches or astrology or lucky numbers and lose great bunches of money, their jobs and their wives and their kids. The pros play it cool and play the odds, and even they get casually flicked off the coatsleeve of fate from time to time. Perhaps the most dangerous thing about horse racing is that it can give you the feeling that it's possible to know what you're doing and make money at it. Sometimes people do make money, but the most prosperous people at racetracks are probably pickpockets.

Normally, I wouldn't take the chance of being spotted snooping by the person I'm snooping on, but with the funeral today, it seemed a safe bet our Mr. Berenson wouldn't be here.

Besides, I had stopped two towns down the coast and purchased a cheap blond wig. The bad thing about being a redhead, Jake Baronian had pointed out to me early in our association, was that everyone remembers red hair. The good thing, he added, was that's *all* they remember. While trailing targets, and in stakeout situations, I sometimes found it convenient to change my apparent hair color to prevent being too recognizable. Clothes also make the woman, so I spent a few bucks of Val's money on something meek and mild that suited my present purposes.

Val had gone to the gallery already when I got up, but had left me a note that said not to worry about her. She would be attending the funeral at one o'clock with some other local businesspeople, and would see me tonight sometime. I decided to take her word for it and not worry about her for the time being.

Instead I worried about Tony, and about what the police might be finding out that I had no way of knowing. I worried about his total lack of alibi for the time of the shooting, and the highly convenient burglary of a few nights previous, which would certainly be one way to set up "losing" a gun. It would be impossible to prove one way or another, since most stolen property doesn't conveniently reappear anyway, but it didn't help his case with the police, and if it came to a trial, it could put a lot of suspicion into a jury's collective mind. Juries are instructed to make their decisions based on evidence only, but they're also made up of a dozen fallible human beings, and I fervently hope my life is never in the hands of one.

Of course, the police were knocking themselves out to find anyone who could positively place Tony across the street from Chandler Stone's office last Wednesday night. He had plenty of motive, judging by his words on the night of the argument, and even Tony didn't deny he threatened to kill Stone, which could be used to prove intent.

Tony was still keeping mum, evidently to protect someone else, and he didn't seem to care how many people, myself included, were going bananas trying to keep him out of jail. I decided that old friend or no, I would lots rather be on a case whose principal cared whether or not he got off the hook.

I turned across the coast highway to the county fairgrounds entrance, another fantasy in the Spanish style. Tall palms waved over the gates to the racetrack, and the sea was close enough to tinge the air with salt. I found a parking spot not more than half a mile away, paid my money along with the rest of the suckers, and went in.

Down around the betting windows, where the porters lose ground by the minute against the litter of cigarette packs, racing forms, and losing tickets, seemed a likely place to find people who know people. Armed with a picture cut from a brochure I had taken from a little lucite holder on Crystal Kramer's desk, I walked up to a man dressed in khaki chinos, worn loafers, and a white shirt.

"I was wondering if you could help me." He was eight inches taller than I was, so looking small and helpless was not a problem.

"Sure, little lady. You need a good tip on a horse?"

"Thank you, but I'm not here to bet. You see, I'm looking for my husband."

"You should have him paged. Did he go to make a bet?"

I drew inward in feigned embarrassment. "Oh, no, nothing like that. I haven't seen him for over a year. Not since he left home." Here I allowed my voice to break slightly. "Someone told me they saw him here earlier this month, and I was just wondering . . ." I had cut out the picture of Berenson's smiling face and laminated it, hoping it would pass for a personal photo behind the faded plastic of my wallet picture holder. I passed it to the man, who looked at it and shook his head.

"I don't know—I see so many guys down here during a season. You need to ask Whitey." He scanned the crowd. "There he is—the guy in the green jacket and yellow pants. He never forgets a face." He pointed out the sharp dresser standing about twenty feet away and assured me he would be able to help. "But if you never find the guy, lady, I think you're better off, know what I mean?" I certainly did.

Whitey was my man, all right, and my poor deserted wife act brought me all the information he had on the low-down bastard who had run off to spend all our savings on the horses. It seemed Berenson was never far from Del Mar on any weekend in the season, was a big bettor and a bigger loser. He was into some large unpleasant men for six figures, and Whitey didn't expect to see him around until he came up with it. He advised me not to cancel any standing insurance policies.

On the other side of the bleachers, I could hear the first race going off. I consulted Mickey. Post time, also, for Chandler Stone. The stands groaned as a few thousand screaming race fans stood up to cheer on their choices. Most of them were going to be awfully disappointed in about two minutes. The rest would be on their way down here to collect their earnings. I decided to be gone when they got there.

CHAPTER 10

. . . .

DROVE BACK UP TO MORADO BEACH FEELING FOR THE FIRST
time like I might really be onto something. I stopped at a gas
station and changed, stowing the wig and dress in the trunk of
my car. After lingering over lunch at a sidewalk café and catching up on my tourist watching and T-shirt reading, I decided
to drop by and pay my respects to Barbara Stone at the *après*
funeral gathering. As long as I was there, I'd see what I could
dig up about the late Mr. Stone, too. I called ahead. Barbara
recognized my name when the maid passed it on. I felt like a
creep knowing she probably wouldn't have wanted to see me
if I were a stranger, but goddammit, I couldn't help it if I knew
practically everyone associated with this case. I wasn't sure if
it was going to end up hurting more than it helped, but what
difference did it make? I was here, and I was the detective.

I pressed the button on the ugly little gatepost that did
security work for the palatial Costa Azul estate of the late
Chandler Stone. It beeped at me, and the double wrought-iron
gate swept slowly open in front of my car. I moved forward
along the wide asphalt drive, and the gate swung shut again.

Up ahead, a three-story pink stucco villa that looked a lot
like Stone Towers, Stone West Mall, and several dozen other
building projects I had seen along the coast the last couple of
days showed itself from between the double row of carefully
groomed cypresses that lined the road leading up to it.

A vast lawn spread all around, comprising more acreag than most small housing developments, and in the distanc an old Mexican man squatted next to a pile of hand too and tinkered with some sprinkler controls. Two or three turn later I came to a flagstoned parking area already occupie by a white Cadillac with impenetrably tinted windows, and recent-vintage Jaguar in British racing green. I pulled in by th Caddy and got out of the car. I had expected the driveway to b full of cars, and the house full of people, participating in th usual post-funeral buffet and gabfest that I've always found s difficult to comprehend. It would appear the send-off luncheo was occurring elsewhere, and my hopes of blending in whil overhearing choice bits of conversation were dashed.

The view from this side of the house was of the valle landward of Morado Beach, a picturesque landscape of rollin hills, just starting to turn golden from the heat, and contrast ing clumps of dark oak trees. Here and there an expensiv neighborhood of white stucco and red tile crept up a hill c down into a valley. I wondered how much of his eastern vie Chandler Stone had owned before he died.

The ocean was just down the hill from the other side o the house, providing a completely different view to the wes I experienced a pang of envying these rich women I knew.

The pang returned when I was led inside Barbara Stone' first-floor living room. Spanish Colonial furniture, certainl authentic and terribly heavy-looking, lined the walls, leavin the floor largely open to a huge Mexican rug and a beautifull waxed red tile floor that looked as if no one had ever walke on it. All of the art on the walls was by Tony Garza—scene of vivid deserts and impossible skies and dark-skinned peopl in beautiful bright clothing. I had never seen so many togethe in a single place.

"Señora will be right here," said the maid, who went as fa as the door and hovered, as though she shouldn't leave m alone with the ashtrays.

There was a clattering sound from the next room, and th sound of cursing. The maid hurried out. I followed.

Barbara Stone had fallen down part of a flight of stairs an was sitting in an undignified pose on the landing, the hig heel of one shoe broken completely off. Her hair looked lik it hadn't been combed that day, and her face had the mushy look that usually comes from several days of dedicated alcohol abuse. I assumed she had not attended the funeral.

The maid shot me a look, as if to chastise me for witnessing this, and hurried up the stairs to Barbara. Murmuring in Spanish, she helped her to her feet.

Barbara gripped the banister and turned her face toward me. A large bruise, purple fading to green, covered her right cheekbone.

"I'm afraid you're not seeing me at my best, Caley," she said, her words a bit muddled. The odor of liquor floated down at me; I wondered about the wisdom of mixing it with whatever her doctor was giving her. She slipped out of the shoes and handed them to the maid, descending with alcoholic caution in her hose.

She wore a long-sleeved dress in spite of the warmth of the day, and the maid rushed to finish zipping it up for her. As she reached the bottom of the stairs, she held out her hand and I shook it. "It's been a long time since I saw you last," she said. "Fifteen years? Sixteen? That was a long time ago. Andy was just a little boy. What brings you back to Morado Beach?" She walked toward the living room and I followed.

"I came back for the high school reunion. Fifteenth. I'm going to be in town for a few days yet. I saw Andy yesterday." I could hear myself lurching through my part of the conversation. It was appalling.

"Andy. Yes." She smiled. "He was here this morning, I think, but I was sleeping." The smile faded slowly, as though she had forgotten the thing that had brought her pleasure. "The doctor gave me some medication, and I'm only supposed to take it at night, but the days have been so awful." She gazed at a point on the drapes and shook her head.

"Yes, I know. I want to offer my deepest sympathy. I've talked to a lot of people who were acquainted with Mr. Stone, and he seems to have been much admired." That was technically the truth, I figured.

She sat down on a sofa and gestured for me to sit, too. "Oh, yes, he was." She frowned. "Not by Andy, of course, but he had many friends."

It was disturbing to me to see her like this. When I was in high school, Barbara McCain had been someone I looked up to. She and Brian were partners in their own law firm, active in liberal politics and conservation issues before that was utterly hip. They knew the best and brightest people, and had a brilliant future laid out for themselves. Back then, I couldn't think of anything I wanted more than to be just like her.

For herself, Barbara had seemed to regard me as the younger sister she never had. She was always willing to talk to me and, more important, to listen. She gave me armloads of clothes, taught me how to dress, and never treated me like a servant just because I sat for her kid.

So many people have said "You can't go home again"; it's become a hopeless cliché, but it felt very true to me as I sat there looking at this woman I had so admired, and seeing what she had become. I wanted to do something for her.

I pointed to the bruise on her cheek. She had put layers of makeup over it, but it would have been impossible to hide. "You ought to try ice for that."

Her hand flew up to her face and flitted about the discolored area without touching it. "It's this medication. It makes me dizzy. I fell down this morning and did this, you know. I feel so clumsy." She fell silent for a full minute, her hand still poised beside her face.

There was no use making any more small talk. Much as I dreaded it, I decided it was time to jump in and get down to business. "I know this is a difficult time for you, but I didn't come here only socially—there's another reason."

Barbara tilted her head, confusion filling in some of the emptiness in her eyes. Her hand fell down to her lap. "What reason?"

"I'm a private investigator, Barbara. I've been hired to look into some of the facts concerning Mr. Stone's death. It would be helpful to me if you'd agree to answer some questions." I spoke slowly, hoping it would sink in. It sunk in.

"How dare you," she began, and the fog began to lift from her face, replaced by simple anger. "Chandler isn't even in the ground yet. How dare you intrude on me like this!"

She rose, still unsteady, and I stood up in self-defense. This didn't seem like a good time to mention that Chandler had been in the ground for about an hour and forty minutes.

"It's not enough the police come here, with their questions and their suspicion, now I can't even let someone I know in the house." She turned and walked toward the stairs, showing real purpose in her movements for the first time. "Elena, show Miss Burke to the door."

I started to follow, but Elena barred the way. "Barbara," I called after her as she headed for the stairway, "I'm terribly sorry. I didn't mean to make you angry, but I really need your help in this."

"I can't help you," she said, negotiating the stairs slowly. "Please leave now."

"Señorita, *por favor*," Elena said, not entirely unkindly.

"Barbara, please!" She turned around and regarded me from the staircase, gripping the banister rail so tightly that I could see white around her knuckles. "God, I'm so sorry. I was too abrupt; I should have found another way to say that."

"It doesn't matter," she said, shaking her head. "I just can't talk about it right now. To anyone."

"It's important. Please say you'll talk to me—if not now, then some other time. Just tell me when. Someone's life may be at stake."

"My husband's life is over," she said. "I can't talk to you. Please just leave."

Elena opened the front door and stood beside it expectantly.

"I'm coming," I said. I shouldered my bag and walked out into the May sunshine. The door closed behind me.

I had come away with nothing—not a totally uncommon occurrence in my line of work, but irritating just the same. I'd been doing this long enough to know, however, that what seems like nothing in the short run seldom is in the long. People frequently give you the most information when they're trying not to give you any at all.

I needed to get some distance from the situation, and a fresh perspective. Andy might be able to help with that, I thought. And maybe he could help me figure out how to make amends to Barbara, too. I had accidentally trampled an old friendship that had meant a lot to me, and I needed to set things right.

I got back in the car and traveled the half mile of interstate that called itself a driveway. When I reached the gate, I pushed the button on the inside security post. It buzzed at me—an electronic raspberry.

"Okay," I said to the post, "so I blew it."

CHAPTER 11

· · · · · · · · · · · · · · · ·

HOT SURF WAS TOWARD THE SOUTH END OF TOWN ON MORADO
Boulevard, between a custom surfboard shop and the Crow's
Nest Cocktail Lounge. I walked up the wooden steps clutching
a large manila envelope under one arm, pausing to look at a
rack of T-shirts on the porch. Inside, a sun-bleached boy in a
Day-Glo shirt stood in front of a baseball game on a portable
TV, helping out the batter with some expert body language.

"Excuse me."

The boy stopped in midswing and turned around. A patch
of hot pink skin grew on his nose and cheeks, under a peeling
layer of dark tan. He smiled a smile out of a toothpaste ad and
shrugged apologetically. "Hey, I'm sorry. Big game today."
He pointed at the TV. "Only I have to work. Can I help you
with something?"

"I'm not here to buy anything. I'm looking for Andy. If you
could just tell me where to find him, I'll let you get back to
your game."

"Out there." He pointed out the open back door to the ocean.
Out beyond the breakers I could see a head full of blond spikes
atop a multicolored wetsuit, in the midst of a crowd of other
surfers.

"Oh, I get it. He gets to play while you mind the store."

"Well, he is the boss."

"And you are . . ."

"T. J." He held out his hand.

"I'm Caley Burke," I said, "an old friend of Andy's. Well, don't miss any more of the game, T. J. I'll just stand out here and hope he spots me."

"Oh, it's simpler than that. I'll run up the flag." He stepped out onto a small, weather-beaten back porch and pulled at a length of cotton rope on a pulley. A bright red flag sporting a skull and crossbones rose to the top of a pole above the store roof.

"Red?" I inquired, pointing at the flag.

"No prisoners," T. J. replied with a grin, and walked back inside. A moment later I heard a muttered "Fuck!" from the direction of the baseball game. Things were not going well for the Dodgers.

A promising swell rose up out there where the big ones come from. Three or four of the surfers pointed to it, and began positioning their boards to be in the best place to catch it when it got there. Andy and two others caught it in the right place at the right time, and began their ride.

Watching them, it was possible to perceive the wave as a static thing; a solid shape moving toward the shore on a slightly angular course, with three surfboards embedded in it like insects in amber. The illusion was shattered somewhat when first one, then another of the surfers wiped out, flying head over surfboard into the wave, which was water again. Andy rode the wave till it was small and tame, then lay down and paddled into shore. He waved at me from the shoreline and untethered himself, then trotted across the beach with the board under one arm.

"So what do you think?" he said when he had come inside, indicating the store with a wave of his arm. "Is this the place, or what?"

"Since it's the only surf shop I've ever been in, it very well could be," I admitted. Behind the counter T. J. snorted.

"Why don't you go stock a shelf or something, smartass?" Andy asked, stepping out of his wetsuit and throwing it behind the counter. T. J. ducked as it sailed over his head and hit the far wall.

"Aw, come on, it's the top of the ninth, and L.A.'s down six runs."

"Well, then, I guess you'd better keep watching, T. J.—they're going to need all the help they can get. We'll be at the Nest." He turned to me. "The Nest okay with you?"

"Sure."

Andy took off his shirt and tossed it on top of the wetsuit. We stepped out onto the porch and he picked a new one from the rack, putting it on on his way down the steps. We walked across a short stretch of iceplant-overgrown sidewalk to the Crow's Nest and went in.

It was very dim inside, which I think was merciful. There was an abundance of dark wood and dark Naugahyde above a floor littered with peanut shells. The only light besides the rectangles formed by the open front and back doors was a TV set tuned silently to the last inning of the baseball game. Various junkyard treasures of a nautical nature lined the back of the bar, adorned with a quarter inch of dust.

Andy waved at the bartender, who nodded at us. "You feel like a beer? You want a yuppie beer? They have it here. This is a real class joint, huh, Charley?"

Charley grunted.

"Sure," I said. "Beer sounds great. Order whatever."

"Two Coronas with lime, Charley. Clean glasses this time." The bartender flipped him the finger. You could tell this was a regular routine for them.

An old man sat at the bar, leaning forward on his elbows in a pose of anticipation or perhaps anxiety, an empty shot glass and a half-empty bottle of whiskey in front of him.

"You remember Leo Keeler?" Andy said as we sat down in a booth on the other side of the room. A huge bowl of peanuts occupied the center of the table.

I looked again at the man. "Yes, but I don't think I would have recognized him. He looks so old."

Leo Keeler was another town character, a skirt chaser and a drunk without any of Tony's redeeming qualities. He had had a lot of run-ins with angry fathers in his younger days, but managed to avoid getting shot or hung long enough to lose his good looks and most of his wits to booze, so that in his later years he had to make do with women old enough and desperate enough to pick up in bars like this one.

By the time I lived in town Leo was a joke, but on the infre-

quent occasions when he sobered up for a few days, it had
been possible to imagine the dangerous young man he must
have been when he and Tony Garza were best friends fifty
years or so before. Something had happened between them,
and nobody knew what it was, but their friendship had turned
to hate, and neither of them had a good word to say about
the other.

"Does Leo still have that old fishing boat he used to run?"
I asked Andy.

"Yeah, and the damned thing still floats. He lives on it now,
down in the slips by the pier. Only I think he's in a new line
of work."

"Oh?"

"Yeah, Leo leaves town headed south, he comes back, and
after a while there's a whole new supply of shit on the streets.
Not just dope, but everything you can think of—crack, heroin."
He shook his head.

The beers appeared at the end of the bar and Andy got up
to get them.

"Do you have proof he's supplying the stuff?" I asked Andy
when he sat back down. "Have you ever bought anything
from him?"

Andy handed me my beer and a glass. He squeezed his lime
wedge into his beer, then popped the wedge down the neck of
the bottle. "Yuppie in training," he cracked when he saw me
staring at him. I followed suit, ignoring the glass and taking a
swig from the bottle. From a purist standpoint it wasn't beer,
but it was cold and tasty.

"To answer your question," Andy said, "I don't do any of
that shit, but the word on the street is, no matter who you buy
it from, Leo Keeler's the guy bringing it in."

"I wonder if the police know about it."

"You're the detective."

"Right. And I'd better limit myself to one case at a time."

"You want to grill me now?"

"Andy!"

"I beg your pardon." He sat up straight and put on a long,
prim face. "Ahem. Would you care to discuss the Chandler
Stone murder case at this time?"

"Yes, wiseass, I would. I have to talk to everyone, you

know—it's nothing personal. I don't think you killed him or anything."

"Why the hell not? Don't dismiss me so easily, Miss Detective. I could as likely be your killer as anyone in this town. I hated Stone's ass—everybody knows that. So what do you want to know?"

"You were spending the night with your girlfriend last Wednesday night, right?"

"Ex-girlfriend. We spent the night fighting. I left about three. I think I lost the fight."

"Not much chance she'd lie for you then, is there?"

"If you asked her right now, no. I think she'd be happy to see me gassed."

"Then it looks like you're covered. Your dad was out with a woman, too, right?"

"Right. One of the great classic lovers, my dad. Actually, this is only the second time he's shown any real interest in a woman since Mom flew the coop. I'm kind of happy for him. Anything else you need to know?"

"Yes. How to get back in your mother's good graces."

"What's the problem?"

"Well, I don't think she's any too happy with me right now. I went by to see her, and my timing was all wrong. My approach, too."

"She still blitzed on tranquilizers?"

I nodded. "Booze, too, I think."

"Yeah. I've been going by to see her, but she hasn't been home, in a manner of speaking."

"She wasn't all there today, either, but she came to life as soon as I started asking questions, and threw me out of the house. I don't think she made the funeral."

"Me neither. Slipped my mind." He guzzled half the beer. "Hey, don't worry. I'll go over later and talk to her. It'll be okay."

"It was my fault, really. I just feel like total shit. We used to be friends, you know."

"Yeah, well, Mom was a friend of mine once, too. You have to understand about the last seven years. Let me give you the big picture." He took another long swig of his beer and shut his eyes tight for a moment. When he opened them again, there was a coldness in them, like I had seen on the beach when he first spoke of Chandler Stone.

Stone had blown into town, Andy said, and started buying up real estate left and right, setting himself up on the hill in Costa Azul, opening up an office downtown, and getting himself known as a power to be reckoned with, and one hell of a nice guy. He engaged the firm of McCain and McCain to handle his legal affairs, and became a personal friend of the family.

Six months later Barbara announced that she was filing for divorce. It was the first Andy, or Brian for that matter, had known anything was wrong. Brian moved out of the house, which had been a gift to Barbara from her parents, and Barbara and Chandler Stone were married the week after the final papers were filed. Andy didn't think his dad had ever gotten over the shock. It didn't look like Andy had, either.

"Stone knew I hated his guts. It was mutual. We both pretended in front of Mom, but I couldn't stick around and watch what he was doing to her. Mom had signed over the old house to me, and I moved back in."

"What was he doing to her?"

"Oh, just making sure all her needs were met, or creating them in the first place. Uppers in the morning, booze all day to take the edge off, cocaine for those special social occasions, then for any occasion, then for no occasion. Downers at night to get to sleep, then get up and get wired. Every fucking day."

He looked up at me. "If she wanted it, he had it. Well, at first she wasn't that hot for it, but he was doing it, and all his friends were doing it, and I think she felt out of it if she didn't get fucked up right along with everybody else. And Stone was very persuasive."

He cracked a peanut and tossed the shells into the mass on the floor. "It didn't get any better when I moved out, of course. In the past seven years I've watched my mother turn from an interesting, intelligent woman into a zero who only lives for what's in the bag. Whatever that happens to be. She gave up her law practice, she gave up all the important stuff she used to do, she gave up her marriage, and finally her son, all for the sake of getting fucked up and throwing parties for rich powerful people who never cared about anything but getting richer. And can you figure it? Because she wanted to sleep with that rich pig." I watched his fingers tighten around his beer bottle.

I touched his hand and his grip loosened, but his eyes were still hard. "Andy, if the police saw the look on your face right now, you'd probably be elevated to the status of prime suspect, alibi or no alibi."

"But I know I'm not capable of killing anyone," he said, very low. "And the reason I know I'm not capable is because I didn't kill Chandler Stone."

I took a deep breath, and then the plunge. "I believe you. And that means a lot, because I'm going to look like the world's biggest fool if I'm wrong now. So here goes. I've got a proposition for you—would you like to help me find out who *did* kill him?"

He cocked his head to one side, made a gun with his fore-finger. "You mean play detective?"

"Well, it's not as much fun as it sounds, but yes, basically. I need an assistant. The faster I can gather information, the more likely Tony Garza won't be arrested for Stone's murder. That's providing, of course, that he didn't actually do it."

"Of course. Where do we start? Who would you like me to tail?" He smiled wickedly. The old Andy was back.

I handed him the envelope I had brought. "These are copies of all the police reports. This stuff is incredibly confidential."

"So I should read it and then destroy myself."

"Practically. Get familiar with this stuff, but never mention to anyone that you saw it, or that you even know *I've* seen it. Someone had to bend some serious rules to get this to me."

"I'll bet I can guess who that was," he said, giving me an appraising look.

"It's impossible to have any privacy in this town, even when you're just visiting, isn't it?"

" 'Fraid so. So after I read this stuff, what do I do?"

"You talk to people. The argument between Tony and Stone took place in the parking lot of La Romana. That's just north of the state beach, and if memory serves, not far from where a lot of partying goes on on the weekend. It was a Saturday night when all this happened."

"So you think it's possible someone may have heard the shouting."

"That's right. The police have already been to all the houses and apartments on the other side of the highway and have gotten nowhere. Ditto the restaurant employees. A few people heard voices, but no details. If there was anyone down on the beach, though, they may have been able to hear actual words that were said. If I could get someone to come forward, it could be very important. Right now we only have Edmund Berenson's word for what the argument was about, and he isn't exactly unprejudiced."

Andy nodded. "I can do that. Anything else?"

"Well, I've got a list of all the people who were within two blocks of the shooting that night. Not a very long list. Nobody except one guy saw or heard anything. Tomorrow I'll start calling on them to see if their memories have improved, but I don't have much hope.

"The other thing I need from you is to ask around if anyone saw Tony that night on that lousy strip of beach south of the state beach—the one with all the rocks. I know almost no one ever goes there, but . . . oh, shit, what time is it?" I dug in my handbag for Mickey.

Andy consulted a watch the size of a Japanese radio—waterproof to five million feet or so, no doubt. "Almost five. You got a hot date?"

"With a telephone." I finished my beer and got up.

Andy waved at the bartender. "Put these on my tab, Charley. Gotta go."

Leo Keeler was still hunched over the bar, the bottle a lot emptier now. He looked like a man with a big problem, but I don't suppose anyone cared. I knew I didn't.

I checked the answering machine when I got back to Irene's. Michael hadn't called yet. The house was empty, and I didn't feel like staying inside alone. I changed into some shorts and a Hot Surf T-shirt Andy had given me, covered myself liberally with sunscreen, picked up a cordless phone from one of the tables, and took my sketchbook down to the beach.

From the library at the back of the house, French doors led out onto a redwood deck that became a staircase going down to the beach. On each landing was a bench, and at the bottom was a white wrought-iron table and two chairs on a wide lower deck that sat well above the high tide mark. The sun was heading west, going golden, making an interesting play of values on objects. It was a good time to draw.

Only I couldn't draw. While I was busy I could keep my mind off Tony, but when I sat still and tried to empty my mind the way I needed to for drawing, his ruined face was all I could see. This wasn't a stranger—someone I could encounter in passing and forget—this was an old friend who needed my help. I needed to have further contact with him, get him to open up to me somehow, if I was going to help. Only I couldn't bring myself to make that contact.

Maybe Rob was right. Maybe I should drop the case and help Val find someone who was more experienced—and, more to the point, more objective. But not until I'd given it everything I've got; that's what Jake had said. As I sat in one of Irene Hayden's faux Chippendale beach chairs and contemplated the blank paper on my lap, I wondered how much I had.

CHAPTER 12

· · · · · · · · · · · · · ·

"SO IS THIS A MINIMALIST PIECE, OR WHAT?" DAVID'S SHADOW
fell on the empty page and slithered off the edge as he walked
around to the other chair.

"I wish I had even a minimal inspiration right now," I
replied, setting the sketchbook on the table and putting the
pencil on top of it. I didn't want to bring up how upset I was,
because I realized he was a big part of it.

"An artist doesn't wait for inspiration; you know that."

"Yeah, I guess I do. I was looking for an excuse." We sat
in silence for a minute, watching the ocean.

"I rang the bell up at the house. When there was no answer
I thought you might be down here. I hoped you would be."

I looked up at him.

"I'm sorry I flew off the handle yesterday. I had no right to
treat you like that. You're trying to help us, help Tony, and I
go and bite your head off."

"You only got defensive because you thought I didn't
believe Tony is innocent. You were only trying to protect him; I understand that." I didn't look at him while
I said this. I felt very close to tears. I think we're never aware of the extent of hurt feelings until the person
who hurt us apologizes. Then it's easy to lose control
and make a total fool of yourself. I decided I wouldn't
do that.

"Yeah." He shook his head. "I guess I don't have a lot of objectivity where Tony's concerned. He and Valerie are really my only family."

"I understand that. But I need you to understand my position, too. I have to be objective if I'm going to do a good job. If I get it set in my mind how things are, I could totally miss noticing something important that was staring me right in the face."

I was feeling stronger now—talking about my work was a lot safer than talking about my feelings. "That's not so hard to do when you're working with strangers; you just keep a hard shell of suspicion between you and the people you're investigating, and even the people you're working for. When friends are involved, you don't have that insulation."

David reached over the table and picked up my sketchbook. "We were friends once, weren't we?" He began turning the pages.

"Yes, we were." I watched him going through my sketches, the way he used to in the old days, and I felt some of that old breathless anxiety, waiting for him to tell me if he liked them. "I really valued your friendship, and I'm sorry now that I dropped everyone and everything that reminded me of Morado Beach when I moved away."

"Except Val."

I laughed. "Val wouldn't let me drop her. She wrote and she called and she supported the friendship all by herself until I was ready to meet her halfway. But I never came back until now."

"I'm kind of glad you did."

The phone rang before I could think too much about that one. I picked it up.

"Caley, it's Michael. I think I might have something for you."

"Terrific. Let me have it."

"Well, your buddy Stone appears to have been spontaneously generated seven years or so ago. For a guy who's made so much news in San Diego County since he arrived there, he's a total black hole before that, at least on the West Coast. My friend in L.A. did find a reference, however, to an Eddie Bjornsen who was indicted on several federal charges for laundering drug money for some very serious characters down there about eight years ago."

"How serious are we talking about?"

"Family."

"Oh."

"Anyway, some other guy ended up taking a fall, and Bjornsen walked. There was a certain amount of speculation that he may have had to get out of town to avoid some sort of repercussions from his employers. No reference to him since your Mr. Berenson blew onto the south coast. Sound good so far?"

"Sounds terrific. Any pictures I could see?"

"A slew of them. He faxed them up along with the articles this afternoon."

"So what does our Mr. Bjornsen look like?"

"Tall, dark, and handsome. Real matinee idol with a Tom Selleck mustache and curly black hair. This guy probably gets laid more often in a week than I do in a year."

"Probably. Anything else?"

"Yeah. He also went by the name of 'Pony-Boy.' Seems he had a thing for horse racing, and enough debts to keep him lean and hungry. Good with other people's money, but a sucker with his own. Strange combination, huh?"

"Yes, but it's music to my ears, Michael. I don't know how to thank you for this."

"Worth a lunch, do you think?"

"At least."

"Can I fax this stuff to you down there?"

"Well darn, Michael, I left my fax machine in my other pants. Why don't you try sending the stuff to the Morado Beach Police Department, care of Detective Sergeant Robert Cameron, and add a cover letter saying it's courtesy of me. None of it's any kind of evidence as far as this case is concerned, but it does lend a certain amount of credence to my suspicions about this guy. He's apparently the beneficiary of a rather large life insurance policy on the deceased."

"So you think Berenson or whoever he is iced whatshis-name?"

"Stone. And I don't know. It seems too simple, but he's in big money trouble right now. He could have been pretty desperate to get his hands on some cash."

"Well, I hope this does your client some good. You're on for lunch at the Riverport Grill when you get back."

"It's a deal. And thanks again, Michael."

I set the phone down and grinned up at David. At last, a light at the end of the tunnel. If I could put some heat on Berenson, and if he just happened to have killed Stone, the case might be wrapped before the end of my vacation, and Rob and I could start exploring some of those possibilities he talked about. My mood took another swing.

"Good news?"

"The best so far. Edmund Berenson is flat broke, a hundred thousand dollars or so in debt to people who take that sort of thing badly, and had an insurance policy on Chandler Stone's life for enough to cover the debt and take himself out to a nice lunch. He may also be traveling under an assumed name so as not to bear too much resemblance to a certain investment counselor to the mob." I got up from the table and picked up the sketchbook and the phone.

"Jesus, that's great! That's just great!" He came around the other side of the table and hugged me. It took me by surprise, and so did my automatic physical reaction to him; I felt like someone had lit a fire under the soles of my feet. It was a few seconds before I noticed he wasn't letting go.

"I don't think we should get too optimistic too soon," I said, heeding my better judgment and pulling away. "Tony's not out of the woods yet."

David put his hands on my shoulders and looked down at me. "I knew you could help." His eyes were saying a lot, and some of it I didn't want to know.

I took another step back. "That's more than I knew. There are still plenty of unanswered questions, but now the police can ask some of them." I turned away and headed up the staircase to the house. "Want to call Tony from here?" I was getting more confident the more distance I got from him. Being that close to him had completely rattled me.

"I think I'll go tell him in person," he said, taking the stairs two at a time and coming up beside me.

"Just don't get his hopes up too much. The case isn't wrapped just yet. We've made some significant progress, maybe that would be the best thing to say."

"I won't get carried away." He was still looking at me that way.

"I'd better get hold of Rob. He needs to know about this new wrinkle. I wonder if he's still at the station."

David's look changed. "Rob. So are you guys picking up where you left off?"

My face reddened. I hate the redhead complexion that makes my embarrassment so obvious to anyone with two eyes. "What makes you think that?"

"I saw you pulling up to L'Auberge yesterday. I thought then you might be firing up the old romance, but I saw him out alone that night, and Val said you had dinner with her. I guess I'm not too sure what's going on, and I guess it's not really any of my business, either."

We reached the top deck and I opened the doors into the library. "I'm not sure myself. He's interested, I'm interested, but there's this case. We both have to remain objective."

"Objective. Good word. I'll have to keep it in mind myself." He picked up his car keys from a table. "I'm going to go home and tell Tony the good news. And don't worry—I'll be very conservative. Maybe I'll call later, find out any late breaking news . . ." His voice made the last statement into a question.

"Yes. I'll probably be here later. Call me."

CHAPTER 13

. . . .

I HEADED OVER TO THE POLICE STATION AND WENT OVER THE photos and articles Michael had sent down from Cascade with Rob, as well as what I had learned at the racetrack.

"This is all very enlightening, Caley," Rob said, hefting the folder. "We won't know for sure until we can compare prints, but if Berenson isn't this guy Bjornsen, they're identical twins. I'd be fascinated to know what connection Stone may have had to Berenson's former employers. But"—he tossed the folder onto his desk and shook his head—"it doesn't mean he killed him."

"But he *is* broke, he *is* in debt to some very nasty people, he *is* experienced with a handgun, and he *does* have a quarter-million-dollar insurance policy on Stone's life."

"He's also not stupid. Why would he kill Stone for insurance money when both the police and the insurance company would be suspicious of just that possibility?"

"Why would Antonio Garza kill Stone three days after someone heard him threaten his life? He's not stupid either, but he's still your number-one suspect."

"No, Garza isn't stupid, but he is crazy." He lit a cigarette.

"You have two doctors' opinions to back that up?"

"I'm not making a medical diagnosis; I'm making a statement based on my experience."

"In my experience, people like Berenson know people who will come into town and do this kind of thing for you for a financial consideration. They use stolen guns and then conveniently lose them where they'll never be found. The gun *is* still missing, right?"

His eyes flashed. "Would you mind terribly not telling me my job?"

"Sorry, Sergeant. I'm just trying to do mine. I guess I overstepped."

The anger went out, replaced by exhaustion. "Look, Caley, I don't want us to fight about this. This was good detective work, and it turned up something we didn't have yet."

He came around the desk and sat on the corner by my chair. "I promise you we'll follow through on this. We took a set of comparison prints—I'll send them down to L.A. and have them checked against Bjornsen's." His voice softened a little as he leaned toward me. "You could be right. There's not enough evidence yet to place Garza at the scene of the crime; right now we can't even make an arrest. Who knows, Berenson may turn out to be our guy, and if he is, I owe a lot of the credit to you."

He reached out and took my hand, then pulled me up to my feet. "Just between you and me, I hope you're right. I want this case to be closed, and I don't want it to come between us. We have a lot of catching up to do." He dropped the cigarette into an ashtray, then pulled me into his arms and kissed me.

I knew I should be calling a halt to this, but I didn't really want to. "That's what I want, too," I said when I got my breath.

"I wish I hadn't been such an idiot fifteen years ago. I didn't know what I wanted then."

I didn't know what I wanted now. I let him hold me, enjoying the sensations that aroused, but knowing I shouldn't let this develop any further while Tony's fate still hung on the outcome of the case.

Part of me wanted him to ask me to go back to his place so I could plead being swept off my feet. Part of me was disgusted at how ready I was to cop out on my vaunted objectivity for a chance to hop in the sack with my high school lover. Part of me was having a good laugh at the other two parts.

I pulled back. "I think we both still have some work to do," I said, trying to make my voice work.

His hands moved over my back, pulling me closer against him. "Let's get out of here," he murmured into my neck.

"You were the one who said we shouldn't be seen together if I was on the case," I reminded him. "I'm still on the case."

He pulled down the strap of my dress and kissed my shoulder. "You've done what you told them you'd do—you've taken some heat off the old man. They can't expect you to keep going out and digging up dirt on everyone who associated with Stone." His fingers reached for my zipper.

I pushed him away—not the easiest thing I've ever done—and straightened my clothes. "I'm sorry, Rob. I want this, too, but until I feel the case is really closed it would be a terrible mistake."

His eyes blazed anger for a second, then he sighed heavily. "I hate to admit you might be right, but you just might be." He took my hand again, squeezed it hard. "I'm sorry I got carried away. I've wanted you since I walked into that gym the other night and saw you standing there. It was like going back in time. I remembered how it was when we were together."

"It was like that for me, too. But we're not back in time. Things are different now. We have responsibilities."

"I haven't been able to think about mine very much since you got back to town. Will you at least have dinner with me later tonight? I've got an appointment down around San Diego but I could cut it short and be through in time for a late dinner. We could drive down in separate cars. No one would have to know."

"No, Rob." I made my voice firm. Where on earth was I finding all this self-control? "I'm going to stay home tonight, catch up on old times with Val, do something sane. Going to San Diego with you wouldn't be sane."

"Okay. I give up—for now." He raised my hand up to his lips and kissed it.

I pulled the hand away, reluctantly. "Call me tomorrow. Let's not make this any tougher than it is already."

"Okay. Tomorrow."

I left the station as confused as ever about Rob, and pretty nearly everything else. The past had been exerting a powerful attraction over me since I drove back into this town two days ago: everywhere I turned were reminders that I had once called this place home, and some of its people my friends. Had it been a mistake not to come back until now? Had my destiny been waiting here for me for fifteen years while I had been keeping my back resolutely turned to it? Maybe it wasn't too late to take that other road, the one that led to a home and children.

With Rob, that path seemed a possibility for the first time in years. It was frightening, the idea that I might change my life that drastically, yet the idea drew me at the same time. I was filled with images of a different future—a future that included a husband and children. I wished I knew how deep Rob's feelings went, and for that matter I wished I knew more about my own; I'd been working pretty hard at burying them. Getting back in touch with myself was going to be tough, and I didn't need the added confusion until Tony was out of the woods.

The last sliver of the sun was still showing above the ocean as I drove toward the beach. By the time I let myself into the house and walked out onto the deck, it had gone. I wanted it back.

I went back in and played the phone messages. Irene would be attending a benefit dinner in Laguna Beach and staying the night. Russ had to stay late at the office; his mom had the kids and would take them to school in the morning, so don't worry about a thing. Val had some crisis at the gallery and wouldn't be home for hours, sorry—the modern American family communicating. Andy had called to say he hadn't turned up anything yet, and to ask for the latest update. The last call was from David.

"Thought I'd check and see if you were back, yet. Tony's gone to bed already—he seems to sleep a lot these days. I'm restless—I don't feel like sitting around here. You want to go out and get something to eat? I'll call back."

I didn't feel much like sitting around either. After calling Andy and filling him in on the day's information about Berenson, I leaned back in a pile of cushions on the sofa and tried to read a book, tried not to think about Rob and missed opportunities, tried to pretend I wasn't waiting for David's call. Fortunately it wasn't long in coming, because I wasn't being very convincing.

"So would you like to go out?"

"More than about anything. I promised myself I'd stay home, but it's killing me. Where did you have in mind?"

"The Seaside."

"Wow." I'd never been able to afford the Seaside.

"I'm an artist, but I'm not exactly starving. Except maybe for some lobster."

"Sounds fine, then. I'll meet you there. Half an hour?" I hung up and contemplated my wardrobe, among other things. What to wear to the Seaside Hotel was a minor consideration next to whether I should be going there at all. Spending an evening with David appealed to me more than it should, especially after what had just happened with Rob. It didn't seem like my life needed the extra complication, but then refusing a dinner invitation with an old friend wouldn't go very far toward making life simpler, would it? Thus rationalized, I went upstairs to change.

CHAPTER 14

THE SEASIDE HOTEL WAS ONE OF THE OLDEST BUILDINGS IN Morado Beach. It overlooked the Pacific from a slight rise at the far northern end of town, amid grounds landscaped like a European villa, which it resembled. A rose garden occupied the hill behind it, and at the base of the hill a pier jutted out into the ocean. The pier had been a popular fishing spot in days gone by, frequented by retired and unemployed locals, kids, and others with no place else to go. At the end of the pier on either side were slips where fishing and pleasure boats docked.

A few years ago, according to local tourist brochures, the hotel had been scheduled for demolition. The cost of remodeling it to current standards would have far exceeded its value to a prospective buyer. Several buyers had expressed interest in the real estate, but the worn-out old hotel that had stood since the turn of the century would have to be torn down to make way for completely new construction.

As in most of these cases, a group of local citizens had organized a "Save the Seaside" campaign, and as in most of these cases, it was far short of the money it needed to buy the property.

It had been Chandler Stone, then new to the community, who had stepped in and made an offer that completely outstripped the competition, promising to restore and reopen the old hotel in all its past splendor.

Now the Seaside was the jewel in the crown of Stone's south coast holdings, and from that day on Chandler Stone was a hero to the locals. The local newspapers never missed a chance to photograph him at a civic function, and his political base was broader and stronger than the mayor's, though he never threatened the local political establishment by running for office.

A portrait of him hung in the lobby, looking thoughtfully down on the whole operation from an ornate gold-leafed antique frame under a brass lamp.

It was a very good portrait. At the surface level was an excellent likeness, but beneath that was the force of the subject's personality. The artist had captured the intensity of those piercing gray eyes, and they seemed to be trying to pin me to the plush oriental carpet as I walked up to it. There was something familiar about the style.

"The sainted Chandler Stone," David said from right behind me, "sat for that portrait in one nineteen-hour session that nearly killed both of us. He refused to set aside more than one day for the job."

I turned around. David had abandoned his usual uniform of faded jeans in favor of a pair of pleated gray trousers and a matching shirt of raw silk. I caught myself staring.

"Shall we?" He took my arm and we walked into the dining room.

David had reserved a table at the window and we looked out onto the pier, where tourists walked under old-fashioned streetlamps to the fish and chips place at the far end. He cranked open the window and the sharp scent of the sea drifted in. The fishing boats had come in earlier, around sundown, and the day's catch was being cooked tonight at the local restaurants, including this one.

"The lobster here is incredible," David informed me.

"It equals my weekly grocery budget," I replied, scanning the right-hand column of the menu. "It would have to be."

"I'm picking this one up; you should have the lobster."

For some reason I felt defensive about it. "You don't have to carry me—I was exaggerating about my grocery budget."

"I know that. I want to buy you dinner. I've wanted to buy you dinner since 1976." He pulled a handful of money out of his pocket. "Look, I've been saving up for this for seventeen years; I can afford the lobster."

I sat back, laughing. "I surrender. Buy me a lobster."

We had a bottle of wine with dinner and got a little silly sitting there and talking about old times. Once or twice I caught David staring at me, then he would look out toward the pier for a few moments without speaking. We were discussing our childhoods, always a difficult subject for David, having had Irene Hayden for a mother. He had defied Irene openly to turn to his grandfather when he was sixteen, and she had not spoken to or about him without rancor since, and that about summed up their whole relationship.

Antonio Garza gave David the love and respect he couldn't get from his mother or from his absent father, who meant well but was ultimately unable to cope with sharing his children's lives. David lived in his parents' house like a stranger until he was seventeen, then moved into Tony's spare room and stayed. After that, Val spent as much time as possible at her grandfather's house without making any waves with Irene. David was her anchor.

The lights dimmed. I looked around and saw the waiters clearing away linens and setting chairs up on tables.

"Do you suppose this is some sort of hint?" David asked.

"I'd consider it a possibility." I looked at my watch; Mickey said it was almost midnight. "Should we call it a night?" I wasn't ready to, but thought it would be polite to at least mention it.

"Well, maybe not just yet, but let's move on, anyway, and let these guys go home. How about a walk on the pier?"

David left the money to cover the check, and we went out through the back doors of the restaurant and down a winding path that took us through the rose garden and down the hill to the recently refurbished Seaside Pier.

"Do you remember what this pier looked like when we were in school?" David asked as we walked out onto the artistically rough-hewn planks, under ornate white iron lampposts.

"I even remember what it *smelled* like," I said. "The place was ankle-deep in fish scales, and the 'White Whale' down at the end was a cheap hamburger joint." We passed a picturesque kiosk, closed now, crammed with souvenirs and postcards of

Morado Beach, behind a white security grille. "I think that spot was a fish-gutting sink."

"Another Chandler Stone project." We walked on in silence for a few moments, from one circle of yellow light to the next.

"How's Tony?" I asked.

David laughed. "Actually, about the same. I don't think he's even worried about being arrested. But he's definitely upset about something, maybe the same thing he was arguing with Stone about. When I told him there was another suspect, he just shrugged and said he knew there had to be."

"Has he ever told you what he and Stone were arguing about?"

"Not a word."

"It was about a woman."

"Probably Barbara Stone."

So he knew, too. "No, I don't think so." I thought about continuing, but decided against it. If his mother had been sleeping with Chandler Stone, it would be out soon enough, and it didn't need to come from me.

It was actually very enjoyable just walking out here with David and talking, like we used to when we were kids. I always felt like I could tell him anything back then. Now, I felt like I ought to avoid the subject of Rob Cameron at least.

We stopped and leaned over a railing. Down in the blackness where we couldn't see, the water surged and slapped against the pilings and the hulls of boats.

"Sometimes I think about how much different my life would have been if I'd never gotten to know Tony," David said. "I know Irene would have been happier."

"I don't know. I'm not sure anything could make Irene happy."

"Sometimes I wonder, too," he continued, "if Tony would have loved me as much if I hadn't been able to draw a straight line with a ruler."

"I think he would have. He loves Val, and she can't draw flies."

"Yeah, but he always seemed to think of me as his other self—his other chance—because I was the boy, I guess. I felt responsible to him, and as he got older I started feeling responsible *for* him. When the fire broke out in his studio, I was out of town. Val couldn't get ahold of me until the next day. He was almost dead by then. They didn't think he was going to pull through for the first couple of weeks." He blinked back tears, remembering. "You know he claims the fire was set."

"No. I'd never heard that. Who does he say did it?"

"Leo Keeler—you remember him?"

"How could anyone forget him? I just saw him today, as a matter of fact, at the Crow's Nest."

David grinned. "You hang out in some pretty classy places."

"Occupational hazard. So why does Tony think Leo started the fire?"

"Tony claims Leo's hated his guts for fifty years. They've got some kind of feud between them going back about that far."

"Yes, I remember hearing about it. Fifty years seems like an awfully long time to wait for revenge, though, doesn't it?"

"For you or me, maybe, but some people never let go of a grudge. If he did start it, maybe it was just because he saw the opportunity and decided to act on it."

"Then you think it could be true?"

"I don't know. When you hear Tony tell it, it seems real plausible. The fire investigators say the fire started when a cigarette butt came into contact with some solvent that was stored right behind the easel where Tony was working. It exploded all over him—that's why he was burned so badly."

"Doesn't that seem plausible to you?"

"Tony doesn't smoke when he's painting." It was a flat statement of fact on David's part.

"And do you think Keeler is capable of doing something like that?"

"He's probably capable of almost anything. He told Tony that before he came here he was an errand boy for some tough characters in L.A.—used to do dirty work real cheap because he enjoyed it. I guess he pissed some people off and beat it down here to lay low. It didn't improve his character any.

"Somebody told me that Leo used to make a hobby of getting young girls pregnant; then when their fathers came looking for him, he'd tell them their daughters had been sleep-ing with every guy in town. I could go on and on. Leo Keeler stories are cheap in this town."

"And yet he and Tony were once best friends."

"They were like brothers when they were teenagers. Some-times when Tony gets drunk he tells stories about those times—how they used to go out and get roaring drunk together and play these crazy competitive games. They'd take off their clothes and jump into the surf and see how far they could swim out and still get back; they'd practice shooting tin cans off one another's heads to see who was the better shot. Sometimes I think it's amazing either of them lived long enough to become enemies. But they did. Their paths went wide of one another—Tony became a success, and Leo became a waste of skin."

"What do you think of the rumor that Leo is supplying a lot of the drugs around here?" I asked.

"He's capable, I think—I mean he's obviously low enough—but I don't know if he's smart enough to keep something like that going very long without getting caught."

We walked toward the end of the pier. Even this late, a few tourists remained, walking to the end like us, or coming out of the White Whale, whose neon signs were now blinking out. It was a warm night, and no one seemed to be in any hurry to go anywhere.

When we got to the end, I stopped to lean against a railing. David turned around the other way, and stood looking back the way we had come.

"Sometimes I miss the ocean," I told him. "I only lived here two years, but the ocean got under my skin. I dream about it."

"Maybe you should come back."

"I've been giving it some thought."

"I've never lived anywhere else, except when I went away to school."

"I remember you saying you weren't going to go to art school, that you were going to stay here and learn from Tony."

"Yeah, that was my plan, all right, until Tony had his say. He said if I went to art school, I might be able to make my mistakes quicker than he did and get them out of the way. I argued, of course, but he practically kicked me out the door.

He paid all my expenses for two years in L.A., and when I got back my room looked like I'd just walked out that morning."

"Have you lived with him ever since?"

He shook his head. "I moved out a couple of times, once just last year. I moved in with a woman I met at the gallery. She bought some of my paintings from Val, and we started going out, and after a while I moved into her place." He lifted himself up onto the railing and swung his feet like the seventeen-year-old I could still remember so clearly. "I was going to ask her to marry me."

"And you didn't?"

"She wasn't interested in me; she wanted to sleep with a painter, and be seen at parties with a painter, and live life in the fast lane with a painter."

"Did she find one?"

"Yeah. I introduced her to a friend of mine from art school, and she took off for San Francisco with him." He started to laugh, and I laughed with him.

"David Hayden in the fast lane. That is an image, isn't it?

"Yep. I can't even drink a beer if I'm planning on doing any artwork the same day. Tony's the same way, but it never kept him from staying smashed between paintings. I don't know how he did it. We're not really that much alike, you know."

"You mean you're not keeping half a dozen women happy while their husbands are out of town?"

"Not even one, right now. No, I paint, and I travel a bit. I teach a class, did you know that?"

"No, but I'm not surprised. You were always patient with me."

"You were very talented, even then. Those were excellent sketches I saw today." He stopped and looked at me. "Why aren't you doing something professionally?"

" 'Art is a continual process of self-discovery and self-disclosure.' You said that to me once."

"You remember something I said that long ago?"

"You'd be surprised how much I remember. Anyway, I think I balked at the self-disclosure part. I don't face rejection well."

"If you couldn't get over that, maybe it was because you didn't want it bad enough."

"Maybe that was it. I still carry a sketchbook, though. I never got over that habit."

He stood down from the railing. "I'd like to paint you. I wanted to paint you back then—back in school—but I wasn't good enough then to ask. Now I am. May I?"

"Do I get to keep my clothes on?"

"I'll take it under consideration." He glanced at his watch. "What do you say we head back, now?"

He took my hand and we walked back up toward the Seaside. The sky turned a murky orange. Before I had time to note this, I was torn loose from David's grasp as a huge hand picked me up and slammed me down again. I heard screaming and shouting from somewhere behind me before it all slipped away.

CHAPTER 15

· · · · · · · · · · · · · · ·

THE LIGHTS WERE TERRIBLY BRIGHT, AND SOMEONE WAS ASK-
ing me questions, the same ones over and over again. "I really
wish you'd just go away," I told them.

"Yes, Ms. Burke, you've said that several times already."
The voice sounded amused. "Do you know why you're here?"

"Of course I do." I shook my head. "No. Why am I here?
Where's here? Have I asked you that before?"

"Oh, a couple of times. There was an explosion at the pier
and you were hurt, but not seriously—just some scrapes and
bruises, and a couple of stitches. Do you remember anything
that happened?"

For the first time it occurred to me that I could turn my
head and see who was talking to me. It was a uniformed cop,
a very young one. He was wearing a khaki uniform with a
knife-edge press and a little black tag that read FITZPATRICK.
His eyelashes were very pale around his pale blue eyes. I knew
him from somewhere.

"I'm not sure. It's sort of like a dream, you know?"

"Yes, ma'am. That's pretty normal in your condition."

"I'm cold, Pat." Of course, it was my buddy Pat. "Can you
get me a blanket?"

"You've got one, ma'am, but I can get you another one."

I looked down at the striped flannel hospital blanket. "Oh
of course."

98

"Just you wait here and I'll be right back." He pushed aside a white curtain and disappeared.

I didn't seem to be going anywhere. I couldn't even remember where I'd come here from. I was beginning to be aware of generalized pain. I thought about this for a minute, none too clearly, and Pat reappeared with a warm blanket, which he proceeded to wrap around me as if I were a child he was tucking in for the night.

"I think they're going to keep you here tonight," he told me, "but I'll come back and talk to you tomorrow morning. By then we should be able to communicate a little better. You try and get some rest."

"Okay."

"Oh, and Sergeant Cameron called me on his car phone to check in just before I came over," he told me. "He'd heard about the explosion on the radio, but he didn't know you were involved until I told him. I think he'll be here to see you as soon as he can."

That sounded good. "Thanks, Pat. Is it still Sunday?"

"Well, technically it's Monday, ma'am, but it never seems like the next day to me until I've been to sleep."

"Me, too. Good night, Pat."

"Good night, Ms. Burke."

He went back through the curtain and I heard his steps receding, then a swinging door going *whump . . . whump*. Other sounds began to make themselves clear as I became more alert: some moans, a low conversation between two or three people, the clatter of metal on metal.

I raised my eyebrows and located the stitches he had mentioned by pure accident. The pain brought it back to me very suddenly. I sat up. "David!"

A paramedic whipped back the curtain and was at my side instantly.

"Everything's fine, Ms. Burke," the medic said. "Your friend's just coming out of X-ray, and that's where you're headed next."

"Will I be able to see him?" The memory kept looping in my mind of David's hand tearing away from mine and not knowing where he was. Suddenly it was very important to see him with my own two eyes.

"I'll try to arrange something before you go up to your rooms. Oh, and a Ms. Hayden was here to see you a while ago, but you weren't receiving at the time. We talked her into going home after she talked to her brother. She'll be here tomorrow—probably to take you both home."

For the first time I noticed the roaring in my ears, like the ocean had come and stayed.

They x-rayed me and plundered me for various bodily fluids before assigning me a room. More than a dozen people had been injured in the explosion that had thrown David and me ten or fifteen feet before flattening us against the pier. Most, like us, were in relatively good shape, but a few were seriously injured. All the double occupancy slots were taken, and I lucked into a private room. Not for the first time I thanked Jake Baronian for the generous hospitalization policy that went with my job.

They wheeled David and me into an alcove and went away and left us there for a few minutes. He smiled at me out of a face that looked like irate bikers had been playing soccer with it. "Are you all right?" he asked. "They told me you were, but I wanted to be sure." He reached out and found my hand.

"Nothing broken. Of course I feel like shit, how about you?"

"That about covers it." He nodded and winced at the sensation. "I'll bet we'll feel worse in the morning."

"Did anyone tell you what happened out there?".

He shook his head and winced again. "An explosion on the pier. I think I could have told them that much. Other than that, no one seems to have any information—or none they'll give me, anyway. Val was here."

"They told me."

"She's going to spend the night at Tony's—keep him calmed down. He wasn't home the first time she called, but when she got hold of him, he was pretty upset." He reached across and took my hand. "I'm really sorry you had to be there. If we hadn't gone down on the pier, we could be home in bed right now."

I blinked.

"Different homes, different beds." He squeezed my hand, then let it go, slowly. The nurse's timely return made it unnecessary for me to find something to say.

"Your room is ready, Ms. Burke," she announced. "Someone is coming by to get you, too, Mr. Hayden." She grasped one end of the gurney and began to push.

I tried to turn my head to see David, but we were around the corner before I could manage it. "See you in the morning," he called. The nurse wheeled me into a dimly lit room.

More than anything I could imagine right then, I wanted to sleep. I wasn't planning on dreaming, either, but at some point I found myself in the middle of this convoluted scenario about Rob. We were at the beach, and he was mad about something and I didn't want him to be mad at me.

"You said you weren't going out tonight," he said. "You said you were going to stay at Irene's." I tried to tell him it was a spur-of-the-moment kind of thing, but the sound of the waves kept drowning out my voice. After a while I couldn't hear Rob's voice, either, but I could see his face, pale and upset. When I woke up, my ears were still ringing.

CHAPTER 16

· · · · · · · · · · · · · ·

THE PHONE RANG AND I TURNED OVER WITH SOME DIFFICULTY to answer it. I was back in Val's room at Irene's house, and my body felt like it had been steamrollered and backed over. My brains were scrambled and I was flying on Valium and painkillers. The phone jumped out of my hand twice on its way to my ear, but I finally managed it. "Hello."

"Caley, it's Rob. I came by the hospital last night, but you were sleeping. When I came back this morning, they said you'd checked out. Are you all right?" He sounded genuinely upset.

I closed my eyes and propped the phone between my head and the pillow. "Hey, don't worry about me. There's nothing wrong with me that a week's sleep and half a pound of controlled substances won't fix. Besides, the hospital's overcrowded. They were secretly glad I wanted out of there. Valerie said a boat blew up, down at the end of the pier. Was anyone killed?"

"Only Leo Keeler. It was his boat."

My eyes banged open. "Jesus. Propane?"

"No, dynamite. I was out of town. When I checked in on the car phone, Pat told me about the blast. I didn't even know you'd been involved until hours later. Christ, Caley, you could have been killed . . ." His voice broke and he stopped talking.

I smiled to myself. It took me fifteen years, but the guy was gone on me. "I've walked on that pier a hundred times, Rob. No one ever blew it up before last night." Then it struck me. "Jesus, Rob, Leo Keeler! I just saw him yesterday. Someone was telling me that they thought he was dealing drugs here in town. Large quantities of serious drugs. Do you think there could be some connection?"

"Who told you that?" He sounded pissed.

"Sorry—have to protect my sources. But he seemed quite convinced."

"Well, I have to admit it's not the first time I've heard the rumor, but think about it for a minute, Caley; someone in a position like that has a choice of life-styles. Why would he live on a smelly fishing boat instead of a condo on the beach?"

"I never thought about that. I guess you're right, though; if I were supplying the town with drugs I certainly wouldn't live like Leo Keeler."

"That's right. And you wouldn't dress like Leo, and you wouldn't *smell* like Leo. This guy would have to be doing what—a couple of million dollars' business a year? And there's one other thing I think you're forgetting, Miss Private Detective."

"Oh, really? What's that?"

"The police. Remember us? We checked out Keeler's comings and goings pretty thoroughly when that rumor first started the rounds—none of his trips ever coincided with an increase in the local drug supply in any meaningful way. I didn't know Leo, except as a sort of town fixture, and I probably haven't said more than 'hi' to him in ten years but I know plenty about him. He had no police record, except for the occasional drunk and disorderly, and no underground drug business. Trust me on this, my love; Leo Keeler was nothing but an old lush."

"Okay. I trust you. And what was that you called me?"

"We'll discuss it at length as soon as this mess is over. Hey, I've got a couple of hours free. Can I come over and see you?"

I shook my head and wished I hadn't. "I look like shit and I don't feel *that* good. I'm going to rest today and see what tomorrow's like. I'll give you a call if I'm up to company, okay?"

"Okay. If I don't hear from you by three tomorrow, I'll call you. Just to make sure you're all right."

"That sounds great. One way or another, I'll talk to you tomorrow." I hung up the phone and replaced it on the nightstand. I could feel myself smiling as I drifted off.

Val came in in the early afternoon with some soup. I tried to sit up, but everything hurt.

"Let me help you, dummy," she offered.

She pulled me up with one arm and stuffed pillows behind me with the other. I groaned just a bit, not entirely for effect.

"Hurts, huh? That's what you get for almost getting yourself blown to bits. To think I used to *wish* you'd go out with my brother. I don't know what I could have been thinking. Oh, and Andy McCain called while you were sleeping. He was awfully worried about you. He'd just found out you were down on the pier when the bomb went off."

"Did he have any messages for me?"

"He was just anxious about you. I told him you were doing fine and not to worry. I like Andy."

"Me, too. What's in the bowl?"

"Albondigas. I went up to Garcia's and picked up a couple quarts to go. Sick people shouldn't have to eat my cooking."

"*Healthy* people shouldn't have to eat your cooking. Thanks for the soup. I think I might actually be a little hungry. Keep me company?"

"I've got another candidate for that job, actually." She set the tray down on my lap. I looked up and saw David in the doorway. He was dressed in jeans and an unbuttoned shirt, no shoes. There was gauze on his neck and chest, covering abrasions, and some adhesive bandages on his face, covering stitches. We made quite a pair. Val gave me a little wave and made a quick exit.

"I thought you'd be home" was all I could think to say. I was glad I didn't know just how awful I must look. I wished I had at least combed my hair since I woke up, but I hadn't had the energy or the inclination.

"I guess I am. Val moved me into my old room next door and told Irene in no uncertain terms she has to get along with me for a couple of days while I recuperate. It's like being in high school all over again, except Tony called at the crack of dawn to make sure I was still alive."

He sat down on the bed and picked up the plastic bottle of painkillers from the bedside table. "I see they've got you on this stuff, too. Works pretty good. I don't think I'd be moving around this much without it."

I scooted my feet back to make room for him, and looked at the large meatball in the middle of my soup bowl. "I've decided I'm not hungry after all. I think I'd just rather pound another couple of those super-pills. Would you take this for me?"

He set the tray down on the floor, poured me a glass of water, and got me two pills.

"I guess you heard about Leo Keeler," I said.

"Yeah. It's all over the papers and TV."

He didn't seem to have anything else to say on the subject, so I decided to drop it. "So is Irene keeping her part of the bargain?"

"Yep. She actually came by this morning and said hello."

"Really?" I couldn't hide my surprise.

"Yeah. Then she took off for San Francisco."

We laughed together, in spite of the aches and pains.

"I guess we'll postpone that portrait sitting, huh?" I indicated my battered face.

He reached up and rearranged a lock of hair over the stitches on my forehead. "No, I think we'll do it like this. 'Caley, in purple and blue.' "

"You're laughing at me," I said, pretending to be injured.

"Laugh back." He pointed to his face, which was less swollen than it had been last night, but still a landscape of scrapes and bruises. Dark whiskers were appearing on his cheeks.

"Doesn't look like you'll be shaving for a couple of weeks."

"I thought I might grow a beard. What do you think?"

I inclined my head and imagined him with a beard. "Might be nice."

"In that case, it's official."

The doorbell rang downstairs. David rose stiffly and went over to the window, which looked out on the driveway. "The police. I wonder what they want."

"If it's the redheaded one, he's here to see me."

"You guys stick together? You have a redhead secret society or something?"

"Yep. We have a handshake and everything."

"Maybe I'd better disappear, then."

"No, stick around—lend me moral support."

"All right." He sat back down on the bed. There was a knock on the door.

I pulled the covers up a bit. "Come in."

Fitzpatrick opened the door, holding his hat. He ducked his head under the doorjamb and smiled apologetically. "Sorry to disturb you, Ms. Burke—Mr. Hayden. I just need to ask a few questions about last night." His eyes went from one of us to the other, as though trying to figure out our relationship. I wondered how much he knew about Rob and me.

"Sit down, Pat." I indicated a slipper chair by Val's old vanity. He eased himself into it, looking like a little kid trying out doll furniture, and took a notebook out of his shirt pocket.

"Both of you were down on Seaside Pier last night at twelve-thirteen, is that correct?"

"Well, my watch said twelve-ten when we headed back to the parking lot, and that's when we were knocked down by the blast," David replied.

"The seaward clock face on the Seaside Pier clock tower was stopped by a piece of flying debris at exactly twelve-thirteen. I believe your watch may have been a few minutes slow, Mr. Hayden."

"It's a lot slower now," David noted. "I smashed it against the pier on my way inland."

I could sympathize with that; Mickey had also been a casualty of the explosion.

"Do either of you recall seeing or hearing anything out of the ordinary before the explosion?"

"No," we answered together.

"We walked down to the end of the pier," David remembered, "then we decided to turn around and go back."

"And what made you decide to go back at that time, Mr. Hayden?"

"Well, we'd walked to the end of the pier, and everything was closing up," David spoke with exaggerated care, as though he were addressing an idiot. "And our choices seemed to be between staying out there, and walking back again."

Pat either didn't notice David's tone, or was ignoring it. "And you noted the time before you started back?"

"That's right. I looked at my watch just before we started back."

"The watch that was several minutes slow?"

David spread his hands. "The only watch I owned."

"You have some experience with explosives, don't you, Mr. Hayden?" Pat looked up from his notebook at David.

"I worked for my father's engineering company for two summers before I went to college. We did a certain amount of demolition."

"Did you learn how to set an explosive charge with dynamite?"

"Well, dynamite's a little old-fashioned these days. . . ."

"But it's still being used for many applications, am I correct?"

"Yes, I suppose it is."

"And it was in even more general use sixteen years ago?"

"Yes, I suppose it was."

"And did you learn to set a dynamite charge, Mr. Hayden?"

"You know, Officer Fitzpatrick, it sounds a lot more like I'm being interrogated than interviewed, here."

Pat closed up the little notebook. "I'm sorry, Mr. Hayden. We're talking to everyone we can place on or near the Seaside Pier at the time of the explosion, and everyone whom we know to have any knowledge of demolitions, particularly dynamite devices. You just happen to be the only person who fits both criteria. Do you want to answer the question?" He smiled disarmingly. "I mean, you're not under arrest or anything."

David let out a deep breath. "Yes, I can set a dynamite charge."

"Thank you. Now I'm going to take a brief statement from both of you if that's all right."

I looked at David. The expression on his face could have been anger. Whatever it was, he was making an effort to bring it under control, but his eyes were bright with some strong emotion. I leaned forward and put my hand over his. He turned up his hand and held on to mine tightly. We stayed that way while Pat asked us the usual routine witness questions, even though we hadn't witnessed anything but our own injuries.

"Well, that about wraps it up," Pat said, closing his notebook with a snap. "I'm sorry to have troubled you folks. I know you must be feeling pretty bad."

"Not as bad as I could be—I'm still in one piece. And by the way, thanks, Pat. It was nice to have a friend there in all the confusion."

He blushed, of course. I'd known he would. "Anytime, Ms. Burke."

He stooped through the door again and was gone.

As soon as he had gone, David picked up the phone and dialed hurriedly. He waited through several rings, then slammed the receiver down. "Where the hell is he?"

"David, what's wrong?" I reached out and touched his arm.

He seemed to come back for a moment as he looked at me. "I've got to find Tony. If the police are on the ball at all, they're going to be wanting to talk to him, too. I want to be there when it happens." He started for the door.

"Wait!" I slid out of the bed and stood up, holding on to the bedpost. "I want to come with you."

"Are you sure you feel well enough?"

"I feel as good as you do."

"That sounds like a good reason to get back in bed to me."

"It'll only take a minute for me to get dressed. Please wait for me." I opened the wardrobe and pulled out some jeans and a shirt.

"I'll put on some shoes and wait outside. We'll have to run Val's blockade, you know."

"I know." I smiled at him. "Thanks." I started to untie the robe, then stopped.

He smiled back. "Guess I'll just wait outside. Hurry, though."

CHAPTER 17

· · · · · · · · · · · · · ·

WE FOUND TONY THREE HOURS LATER, AFTER GOING UP AND down every deserted stretch of beach between his house and Costa Azul. Since Tony had called Val to check on David only a few hours before Fitzpatrick had shown up, and a quick check had not found him at home, David figured he wouldn't be too far away.

Years ago, Antonio Garza had been a familiar sight on the streets and beaches of town. Every day he didn't paint, he spent several hours walking, with frequent stops at his favorite watering holes. Now he did his walking at night when no one could see him, a habit that had cost him an alibi for the time of Chandler Stone's murder. Also, since he wasn't painting anymore, he was drinking nearly all the time, and had the stuff delivered from the liquor store.

If he was upset about what happened, David figured he might have gone to find a piece of beach too rocky and inhospitable for tourists and surfers alike, and settled down to get seriously drunk. There were a number of places like this south of town, and David was sure he wouldn't have walked north, which would have taken him through the heart of the scenic route along the coast and past hundreds of staring people. He was right.

Tony had found a spot on a high cliff overlooking the Costa Azul state beach, and sat down under a cypress tree to kill the bottle he'd brought with him.

He looked so strange and helpless lying there in a patch of the ice plant that covered nearly everything on this part of the coast, surrounded by hundreds of bright purple flowers. He was wearing a long-sleeved white shirt buttoned up to his collar and down to his cuffs. His scarred face looked completely alien atop his neatly dressed body, and the twisted hands sticking out of his shirtsleeves could have—should have—belonged to someone else. His hat and cane, his gloves, and a nearly empty bottle of expensive Scotch lay nearby. I picked them up.

The fog started rolling in while David was carrying him to the car, and the air got suddenly cold and wet.

"I'm glad we found him when we did," David remarked as we got back up to the car. Visibility was shutting down and the air was growing chilled. He loaded his grandfather into the backseat, then climbed in the front and started the engine. "He might have caught pneumonia."

"I still might," I said, cranking up the car heater.

David turned to me and smiled, not without sadness. "Thanks for coming along, Caley. I usually have to do this alone."

I didn't begin to notice how awful I felt until we had Tony home and David had put him to bed. Seeing Tony was a physical shock, and it wasn't one I needed on top of what I had been through the night before. I ached all over and felt too weak to do much besides take some more pills and feel miserable. I lay down on the couch to wait for the medication to kick in. That was all I knew for at least three hours.

When I opened my eyes again, the light was different. There was a blanket covering me. David was sitting at the other end of the couch. My feet were in his lap.

He looked at me and shook his head. "I knew I shouldn't have brought you out. Why did I let you talk me into it?"

"Because you needed a friend." I sat up as best I could on one elbow and tried to defog my mind. "I don't know exactly what's going on, but I gather you think Tony might be in even worse trouble, if possible. If you need to talk about it, we can. Maybe I can even help."

He nodded. "How about something to drink? Some wine?"

I reached in my shirt pocket and pulled out the bottle of pain pills. "I don't think it would mix with these," I said, rattling the container.

"Why didn't I think of that?"

"Probably because you've had too many of these. They make your head funny."

"In that case, let's try to reclaim a few brain cells with some coffee."

"Can I help?" I started to raise up from the couch.

"Nope. No way." He grabbed a couple of pillows from the other end of the couch and arranged them under my head. When he had started a pot of coffee, he came back and lit a fire in the fireplace. I was almost dozing again when he put a mug of coffee down on the coffee table in front of me.

"You don't take anything in this, right?"

"As is, thanks." I scooted up and made room for him to sit. David sat and watched the steam rise from his coffee for at least a minute before he said anything. I waited, not wanting to push him. A kind of gray, neutral night had set in with the fog; it was impossible to tell the time, and only barely possible to see the shape of a car parked across the street. The curtains were open onto it, and the fire was the only other illumination in the room. David got up and closed the curtains. "Do we need a light?"

"No, this is really restful. I like it."

"Me, too." He sat back down, picking up his coffee and putting his feet on the coffee table. "I called Val from the kitchen and told her we'd be late. I can take you back to Irene's anytime."

"Right." I wondered if we would make small talk through a whole pot of coffee.

"When the cops put two and two together, they're going to think Tony killed Leo Keeler, too." David turned and looked at me, gauging my reaction.

I tried not to give away my surprise at this turn of events. It was a professional habit, and one that had no place between friends, but it was such a handy defense, and I used it automatically. I took a deliberate swallow of my coffee, and used up some excess nervous energy leaning forward to put the cup down. "Let me guess. He's been sleeping with Leo Keeler's wife, too."

"I told you, Tony thinks Leo set the fire in his studio."

This time I couldn't hide my reaction and I didn't try. "You're the one they're asking questions about explosives—what do *you* think?"

"I think he's probably right. Keeler was nobody's friend. He hated Tony since they were young men in this town together. Starting the fire wouldn't have been beneath him—I don' think anything was."

"You hated him, too." It wasn't a question. I could see i in his eyes.

"I hated him for Tony, Tony hated him for his own reasons dozens of people have hated him for years. Somebody jus finally acted on it, is all." He drained his coffee. "This may be too cold to say, Caley, but it's just possible that whoever blew Leo Keeler to hell did the rest of us a favor." He picked up the coffee cups and carried them into the kitchen.

Was David capable of doing the world that favor? The question came out of nowhere, and I didn't have time to dea with it before he had come back with refills. I decided to ask a different question.

"Why would the police think of Tony? Does he have demo litions experience, too?"

He nodded. "More than I do. He worked on the freeway crews when he first came to California. They trained him in demolitions because he was small and quick. And who knows—maybe because he was Mexican and expendable. He used to say he learned to be real careful by never forgetting he could lose his hands." He looked at his own hands, artist's hands, as though wondering what his life would mean without them.

"Okay. But where would he get dynamite? He would have to have obtained it after the fire if revenge were a motive, and he wouldn't exactly be inconspicuous purchasing it."

David shook his head. "I wish it were that simple. He had quite a few sticks of some really old, unstable stuff in the shed out back. He bought it when he was helping a friend blast some granite boulders to widen a private road up in the hills somewhere, years ago. He said he kept it because he might need it for something someday. It's like pulling teeth, you know, to get him to throw anything away.

"I kept thinking about it while you were sleeping. At first, I was afraid to go out there and look. I didn't even remember how much he had, really. More than enough to do the job. And my guess is whoever set that charge on Leo Keeler's boat used a lot more dynamite than they needed to get the job done. Personally, I think it was an amateur."

"So did you look to see if it's still there?"

He nodded. "It was there."

"Hold it. '*Was*'?"

"I'm sorry, Caley. I don't want you to be in this deep if you don't want to be. Let's just say it's not there anymore."

I couldn't believe my ears. "Do you have any idea what you've done? You've incriminated yourself, and you may not have done Tony any good by doing it."

"I can't take the chance they might find evidence to use against him."

My head was spinning, not altogether from pain pills. I tried to stay calm. "All right, let's think for a minute, here. Do you really think Tony could have done it? Do you think that was the reason he ran away and got drunk today?" I felt like I was taking an awful chance asking a question like that one, considering what had happened between David and me in this room just two days before. I waited for the explosion, but it didn't come.

"I don't think I really care if he did it," he said, almost too quietly to hear. "I just care that the cops might think he did."

I sat there and willed some blood back into my face. It occurred to me, quite against my will, that the dynamite that blew Leo Keeler and his boat to smithereens could just as likely have come from Peter Hayden's engineering company as from the cache in Tony's shed.

I wasn't sure, right at that moment, whether or not I thought David was incapable of killing someone like Leo Keeler; all of us, I think, have something we'd kill for if it ever came down to it, and where Tony was concerned, David's love and protectiveness went pretty far.

What did seem unlikely was that he would have killed him in such a way as to draw suspicion onto Tony. And, I flattered myself to think, if it had been David who left the surprise package on Leo's boat, he would not have risked my life to make me his alibi. If he would—if he did—then I didn't know him at all, but how many times in my life had I discovered how little I knew someone?

At any rate, I now knew more about all this than I really wanted to. Did David think I would withhold evidence from the police to protect either him or Tony? Would I?

I shook my head to clear that line of thought. What was I doing sitting here by a man I called my friend, speculating on whether he was a murderer?

The habits of investigation are difficult to ignore. One of the first ones you acquire, and for very good reasons, is not believing that anything anyone connected with a case tells you is necessarily true. All my training told me it would be stupid to put the possibility completely out of my mind, yet it made me feel like a traitor, and like David could read my mind as I thought it. I felt like I was going to be sick.

He looked over at me. "I know I shouldn't have said any of this," he said. "I didn't mean to upset you. It's just that we could always talk to each other about almost anything. That's what I remember most, that I could be myself around you."

I decided it was time to act like a friend *and* a professional, if I could manage that trick. "You still can, David. And as long as I'm still on the case, I need to know anything that the police might find important. That way there are fewer surprises."

"What would you like to know?"

I sat up straight and went into detective mode, in spite of the discomfort and the medication. "What did Tony have against Leo Keeler, and vice versa?"

"I don't know."

"Come on . . . they've hated each other for what, fifty years? Both you and Tony think he set the fire that ruined Tony's life, and you don't know what the feud is about?"

David shook his head. "You know Tony. If it's a question of honor, his or someone else's, he can keep a secret forever."

"Is that what he said about it? A question of honor?"

"All I ever got out of him was that he set something right that Leo had done wrong, and Leo never forgave him for it. It involved other people, and Tony wouldn't go into detail."

"And of course you went to the police about Keeler setting the fire, and they couldn't prove anything."

"They said it was an accident. Tony got careless with a cigarette and flammables, they said. I told them he never drinks or smokes while he's painting, but by the time it occurred to anyone to take blood alcohol tests, it was too late to prove he hadn't been drunk, and even that wouldn't have proved that he didn't drop a cigarette. They couldn't prove any human agency besides Tony himself. Tony says the window was open, and he saw someone walk by and throw something in. Then the room exploded."

"He doesn't know if it was Keeler."

"No. He doesn't know it for a fact. He thinks it was, though."

"And he reported his suspicions to the police, and now they know that Tony might have had a motive for killing him."

"Is that pretty serious?"

"Not in and of itself. Motive doesn't prove intent, and neither of those things will link Tony to the crime scene. For that they need someone who would have seen him in the right place at the right time, or some other physical evidence that would place Tony at the scene. If he wasn't there, they won't have that. Barring that, they could possibly use the feud and the dynamite to make a circumstantial case if any evidence of the dynamite survived the explosion, and if the dynamite were the same type used, and if they can find it."

"They won't find it."

I sighed and shook my head. "And access, which probably wouldn't be a problem for anyone. Anyone in town could have climbed on Leo Keeler's boat and planted a prepared charge."

"But not anyone in town could have prepared the charge in the first place."

"Right. That does narrow it down a bit, but it doesn't eliminate all other possibilities. Some people still hold to the theory that Leo Keeler had some connection with the local drug supply. That's something that can get you dead, too, if you get the wrong people pissed at you."

"He was certainly capable of it," David said. "I guess if there were any proof, the police would have burned him down, though."

"That's exactly what Rob said. He also said Keeler's lifestyle didn't exactly fit with someone who was probably turning over a couple of million dollars in drugs a year. What would he be doing living on that scuzzy boat, if he had that kind of money?"

"No, it doesn't exactly fit, does it? Of course he was known to disappear for days and weeks at a time."

"Yes, but the times he was gone and the times he came back never coincided with the drug influx."

"According to Rob?"

"Yes. I mean, he would be the one to know, wouldn't he?" Why did I get defensive around David whenever the subject of Rob came up? I made a mental note to stop doing that.

David got up and put a log on the fire. "I wish I knew how worried I should be."

I wished I did, too.

"I mean, how important can the police even think Tony's connection to Keeler was?" David said. "They haven't even been by here."

"Shit, I must be slipping!"

"What's wrong?"

"Maybe they *have* been here. Maybe they've been here all along. Take a peek out the window and tell me if there's a car parked across the street."

He crossed to the window and pulled one curtain aside slightly. "Yeah. I can't tell much about it in the fog, but there's one there."

"How about the people in that house? Do they usually park out on the street?"

"No, they have a big garage. Even if they had company, it seems like the driveway would fill up before someone would park on the street. It's hard to tell in this light, but I think there might be somebody in the car."

"When you . . . did whatever with the dynamite, did you leave it in the car, or go out to the front at all?"

"No. I took a walk inland from the backyard."

"You wouldn't like to tell me where?"

"You can't get in trouble for something you don't know."

"I already know enough to be in deep shit, but never mind that now. There was a car there a while ago, before you closed the curtains. I'm not saying it means anything, but it could be surveillance. They might just be watching to see where you or Tony will go if you leave the house. Or me, for that matter."

"You mean because you're here with me?" David lowered the curtain and frowned.

"Well, don't take it too seriously. We probably picked up that tail when we left Val's this afternoon, but I don't think anybody really thinks I might have killed Leo Keeler."

He crossed the room and stood in front of the couch. I looked up to see him standing over me. Silhouetted against the fire, I couldn't see his face. His body was easier to read, though. He was clenched like a fist.

"But if they think I did, they could be looking out for you, protecting you from me."

I reached for my coffee. It was cold. I drank some anyway, and tried to keep my hands steady while I did it.

"If that's what they're up to," I said, "they wouldn't be much help out there if you really wanted to hurt me. No, I don't think Rob thinks you killed Leo. If he did, I don't think he'd leave us alone together here for several hours."

"Fuck Rob. I want to know what *you* think. Do you think I killed anyone?"

This was not the time for waffling, for weighing alternatives out loud the way I'd been doing in my mind. This was the time for what they used to call a gut-level reaction, before that term became hopelessly cliché. "No, David," I said, "I don't think you killed anyone." And I didn't, I realized. It was a goddamned relief. I let out a breath I hadn't realized I was holding. I could see some of the tension leave him, too.

"And you think that's the cops out there?"

"If I had a quarter, I'd put four nickels on it."

"How are you feeling?"

"Right this minute? Almost human."

David reached down and pulled me up to my feet. A slow smile formed on his face. "Want to give them something to do?"

CHAPTER 18

. . . .

"I DON'T THINK IT'S VERY GODDAMNED FUNNY!" ROB SLAMMED his fist down on his desk for emphasis, and I winced inside while doing my best to stay totally cool on the outside.

"Don't take everything so seriously, Sergeant. We had to see if the guy was one of yours. I mean, he could just as easily have been a burglar casing the house, couldn't he?"

"Fuck burglars! The guy was there protecting you!" His green eyes flashed. He loomed over me, putting his hands on the arms of my chair, and spoke slowly, separating each word for emphasis. "You were out joyriding with a suspect in the most violent murder this town has experienced in . . . hell, the most violent murder this town has *ever* experienced!" He pushed off from the chair and walked to the window, putting his hands on either side of the blinds and taking several deep breaths. A cigarette was clutched between his fingers, burned down almost to his skin.

"David didn't kill anyone."

"You know that? For a fact?" He dropped the cigarette into an ashtray, and looked back over his shoulder at me, and I couldn't read the look.

"No. Not for a fact. But I know it."

Now I could read the look just fine, but I didn't like it. "You and David getting pretty close these days, are you? Are you in the habit of sleeping with your clients?"

"Fuck you," I said, getting up and picking up my handbag. "If I'm not under arrest, Sergeant, I'm out of here." I turned and headed for the door.

"Caley, wait! I didn't mean that!"

I stopped at the door with my hand on the knob.

"I'm sorry." He came up behind me and put his hands on my shoulders. His chin rested on the top of my head.

I didn't want his apology. I wanted to be pissed off. I tried to maintain the tension in my body, but he drew me close to him and held me. It had the same effect on me it always had, and I could tell it was having an effect on him, too. What was that word, again? Oh, yes. Objectivity.

I pulled away, but not angrily, and turned to face him. "I really have to go, Rob. I'm sorry you were upset by David and me pulling your boy around last night. We decided to go out on a drive, and he decided to follow us. To San Diego and back. It seemed like harmless fun."

"There's no reason to assume David Hayden is harmless. His grandfather's certainly not. If I had one goddamned witness he'd already be behind bars, and if he'd been in jail night before last instead of out on the street, Leo Keeler probably wouldn't be dead right now."

"Why do you think Tony had anything to do with Leo's death?"

He looked at me for a long moment, then shook his head. "I can't tell you everything I know, Caley—you're on the wrong side of this investigation. I've let you have too much information already."

He was probably right, but I didn't feel like admitting it. "You don't know he did it. You don't know he killed Chandler Stone either. And even if you had enough evidence of one to make an arrest, it wouldn't necessarily prove the other."

Of course he didn't have shit for evidence either way, or he would have made a move by now. But I knew if he didn't act soon, the Sheriff's Department was going to muscle in on the investigation, and Rob's ego was fighting that possibility every step of the way. I also knew that if I said any of this to him, he was going to fly off the handle again. I settled on discretion for the moment. "Anyway, I don't think Tony's a killer."

"You don't seem to think anyone's a killer, but two men are dead. Let's make a list of all the people who ever crossed Antonio Garza and see who turns up dead next." His eyes were narrowed in anger.

I wanted to change the expression on his face, make things better between us, but I didn't know how. I reached for his hand and held it. "We always end up fighting about this case, don't we?"

He sighed. "So drop the case."

"I think you know I can't do that."

"You're right. I do know. I won't ask again."

"You didn't ask that time, but let's not split hairs." I took a deep breath and tried to set aside my anger. "I have to do everything I can for Tony—and Val, and David. These people are my friends. I can't let them down just because helping them is proving inconvenient to my personal life or yours."

"Ours," he said, touching my cheek with his hand. "But this isn't going to last forever. When it's over, we'll start again, just like this had never come between us."

"We will," I promised, "as soon as this is over." I stood up on tiptoes and kissed him lightly on the lips. I was out the door before he could react, but I heard him chuckling on the other side. The knot of reporters made a feint in my direction as I stepped out the door, then sat back down when they failed to recognize me as having any connection with the case. Several cursed under their breath, and one slammed a clipboard down hard on the tile floor. These poor bastards were going over the edge, but my day was going swimmingly, at least on the romantic front.

I beamed as I walked past Officer Hogan. She was almost pleasant in return.

I walked out into the south coast spring sunshine, feeling pretty damned good in spite of the aches and pains and the stitches and the medication. How often does a woman get to realize her high school fantasies? How often does your first love come back to you after fifteen years?

CHAPTER 19

· · · · · · · · · · · · ·

I SPENT A COUPLE OF HOURS TALKING TO THE VERY FEW
people who had been anywhere near Chandler Stone's office
around the time of the shooting. Some people recalled hearing
a loud noise, but most didn't associate it with gunfire, and
almost nobody went to the window to take a look. Those
who had, had not been near enough to the crime scene to
see anything. I was beginning to feel as frustrated as Rob
must about the total lack of witnesses. He seemed to want
someone to be able to identify Tony, so he could wrap up
the big unsolved murder and get on with his life. I wanted
someone to identify someone else, so I could get on with mine.
The more I thought about it, the more I thought we might be
getting on with it together. Maybe I'd have that other life after
all—the one I'd almost decided was a girlish fantasy I had left
behind long ago.

After exhausting my pitiful supply of potential witnesses to
Stone's murder, I drove north along the beach, headed nowhere
in particular, thinking about the newest wrinkle in the case.
Whoever had blown Leo Keeler and his boat across a wide
stretch of the blue Pacific had not done me any favors.

It would not be easy to find another connection between
two men as different as Stone and Keeler. One man had lived
in town for more than fifty years, the other was a newcomer.
One kept only the best of company, the other hung out with

people as down and out as himself. They had no friends in common, and only one really conspicuous enemy, and that just happened to be my client. Lucky me.

I spotted the Day-Glo mushroom cloud sign in front of Hot Surf, and decided to stop and see if anyone knew where Andy was. To my surprise he was behind the counter. A rock video was playing on the little TV, minus sound. Andy was watching it glumly. He looked up and smiled when he saw me, then seemed to remember his surroundings and his face fell again.

"Well, now you know how I am," he said, gesturing at the surroundings. "How the hell are you?"

"Lots better than yesterday, thanks."

He came around the counter and hugged me, gently. "You look like shit. So tell me—you get blown up often in your line of work? 'Cause I was thinking about getting a safer night job, like maybe alligator wrestling."

"No, this is a genuine first," I told him, returning the hug. "So what brings you to your own place of business on a day like this?"

"T. J.'s out with the flu. I have to act responsible for a change."

I laughed. "It must be killing you."

"Shit yeah, have you looked at that surf?" He walked over to the back door, which was open to the sea breeze and the sound of pounding waves.

I followed him out onto the little porch. The Jolly Roger was snapping in the wind, but no one was answering the call.

"I tried calling three other people who come in part-time, but no luck. I think they're all out there." He pointed at the pack of bodies and boards that populated the waves.

"Maybe T. J., too?"

Andy shook his head. "Not that boy. He wants to live to be twenty."

I pointed back into the store. "Doesn't look too busy in there."

"Fuck, they're not buying it today, they're out there *doing* it!" He made a gesture of pure disgust at the sight of a dozen bright surfers poised for a wave, and walked back inside.

"Have you considered closing up shop and joining them?"

"Yeah, but the sign on the door says 'open till six.' Somebody's got to be here, and today it's me." He went back behind the counter. "What can I get you to drink?"

"You got any mineral water?"

"Nope. Nothing artificial in it. Coke, 7UP, Orange Crush . . ."

"Coke's fine, thanks." Andy disappeared behind a curtain and I heard a refrigerator door open and close. "What are the odds that Leo Keeler and Chandler Stone could possibly have known each other?" I asked him.

"It's a small goddamn town," he called from the other room, "but knowing the both of them, I don't see how they ever would have met. As far as I know, Stone wasn't even consciously aware of Leo's existence." He reappeared with two frosty cans.

"They were both scum," he continued, "but Stone was real high-class scum. I mean, Stone would be eating lobster at the Seaside while Leo was dripping taco sauce down his shirt at Chihuahuaburger. Leo'd be smoking dope under the pier while Stone was making sure Mom had all the cocaine she needed to stay aloft." He opened my Coke and handed it to me.

"Could they have been doing business with any of the same people, or with each other, for that matter?"

"Not very likely, the way I see it. When Leo was in town and sober—and those two didn't coincide all that often—he'd take charters out on his boat to fish. Mostly tourists, but sometimes locals, too. Stone had his own boat and captain. He wouldn't have needed to use Leo's tub for entertaining clients."

"So how did these two guys piss off two different people badly enough to kill them within five days of each other?" I wondered aloud. "If this were L.A., I wouldn't have trouble believing it. In a town this size, it seems to be bucking the odds."

Andy reached over the counter and lifted over a chair for me. "Why are you assuming it's two different people?" he said, hopping up on the counter.

I sat down. "I don't know that it is, but the methods are so radically different."

"True. But the results are exactly the same. If I wanted to get rid of two people that were in my way, making it look like two completely different murderers just might keep the police from looking for a connection between the two."

"There *is* a connection, you know," I told him.

"There is?"

"You live in this town. Who knew both Stone and Keeler and hated both their guts?"

Andy shook his head in disgust. "Shit. Tony again. Can't that old fart stay out of trouble for a whole week?"

"I'm beginning to wonder. The police haven't got enough to move on it yet, but I don't know how long that will last."

"Could Tony have made the bomb that blew up Leo's boat?"

"I imagine that's what they can't prove yet." Of course I could, but I didn't want Andy to know that just yet. What he didn't know, he couldn't get in trouble for not telling, right?

So did Stone and Keeler have any enemies in common, or didn't they? If Tony or David wasn't the fatal connection, maybe there wasn't one. Or maybe Andy was right, and some mutual associate had cleverly eliminated both of them in radically different ways to throw the police off his trail.

"That still leaves us with having to find a connection between Stone and Keeler," I said. "And it would make my job a lot easier if we did."

"Well, it probably wasn't their tailor," Andy observed.

"Or their hairdresser," I countered.

"They didn't visit the same health club, either."

"Probably didn't even shop at the same stores."

"Ah, no." Andy wagged a finger and took a swig of Coke. "Chandler Stone never shopped. The stores came to him. Custom clothes, custom furniture, custom jewelry."

"Custom drugs?"

"Hm?"

I got up from my perch on the chair arm. "I just remembered what you said about Stone and your mother and the drugs. It's the second time you've mentioned that he kept your mother drug-dependent. Where do you suppose he got the drugs?"

"Well he wasn't hanging around down on the pier making buys, that's for sure."

"Maybe he was dealing directly with whoever was bringing them into town, like he was with the tailors and the jewelers." I began pacing. It helps me think sometimes.

"Which brings us back to Leo Keeler," Andy said. "Also dead, also possibly with a drug connection."

"Unless you believe the police."

"I try not to, but this is your case."

"Rob wouldn't lie to me about something like that."

"Does that mean he *would* lie to you about something else?"

I blinked twice. "No."

"Okay, we'll leave it at that. Hey, don't be mad at me for saying that, okay?"

"I'm not mad." I wanted to be, but it didn't make a lot of sense. Rob had lied to me plenty, back in the old days, keeping me believing in him while he made sure of Melissa, so as not to leave himself with nothing if she decided against coming back to him. He had been so insecure back then.

"So how can we prove the connection?" Andy asked. "Is it possible anything exists to prove they knew each other?"

"Hold it, Junior Detective. We don't know that they did. We only know it's barely possible."

"Three days ago it wasn't even barely possible that Mr. Uptight Edmund Berenson was a mafia money launderer. I mean that guy is such a tightass, he squeaks when he walks!"

"All the best financial counselors are tightasses, Andy. It's one of those amusing facts of life. Criminals need the same kinds of financial advice as the rest of us, only maybe better, to keep them out of jail."

"Well, nothing but the best for my old stepdaddy."

"What did you say?" I stopped pacing under a garishly painted surfboard that was hanging from the ceiling by two pieces of monofilament.

"I said, 'Nothing but the best for . . . ' "

"Oh, wow!" I jumped up and down once. The surfboard wobbled. I took two steps forward to clear it. "It's not what we were looking for, but it's a beginning."

"I'm so glad to hear it. *What* is?"

"Berenson! Who did Berenson work for in L.A.?"

"Criminals. Bad guys. The mob."

"Right. And why have we assumed up until now that he'd changed his ways? He didn't give up any of his other habits, did he? His specialty is laundering dirty money through legitimate investments."

"And Chandler Stone had investments all over the place."

"That's right. And we've always assumed the money came from legitimate sources. Maybe we were wrong."

"So how do we find out?"

"You have access to your mother's house, don't you?"

"I have a key somewhere—I haven't used it for a long time. I can come and go in the big house as I please, I just haven't pleased much the past few years."

"Find time to visit your mother . . ."

"I've been going by every day since Stone bit it."

" . . . And take a look around—drawers, closets, wastebaskets are particularly productive sometimes. I don't know what I want you to look for—anything that will make Stone and Berenson look dirty, for starters; anything that will further incriminate Berenson in particular, and if you could come up with something that would tie Leo Keeler into the whole mess, I'd be in Detective Heaven." I picked up my bag and finished my Coke. "Meanwhile I have a couple of calls to make myself. I haven't been very useful the last couple of days."

"Useful. Jesus, I almost forgot to tell you."

"Tell me what?"

"You had me asking around down on the beach about anyone who might have been near enough to La Romana on the fateful night to hear what was going on in the parking lot. It took me a day and a half, but I finally found somebody."

"Great. Tell me about it."

"Well, there was this couple at the restaurant when it was closing—a couple of locals. They didn't feel like going home yet, so they went down onto the beach to get stoned. A few minutes later they heard some kind of commotion up above, so they walked up closer to have a listen." He frowned and looked away from me.

"Well, what did they hear?"

"Pretty much the same thing Berenson said in his statement to the cops."

"And have we got the name of the mystery woman?"

"Yes, we do, but you're not going to like it." He stood there for a moment, head down, then looked up at me through his lashes. "The name they heard was 'Valerie.' "

CHAPTER 20

• • • • • • • • • • • • • •

I DROVE UP THE HIGHWAY TOWARD TOWN, TRYING NOT TO think. The day was still beautiful, like most days down here; tourists were touring all over the place, and the world was holding on by its toenails as usual. The only thing that was different was the news I'd just heard from Andy.

The road blurred as tears stung me, and I tried to figure out what they were for. Was I disappointed in Val for keeping this Stone thing a secret, or was I angry at myself for being too stupid to see what had been staring me in the face?

Val and I had talked about her marriage over the years, and I knew her relationship with Russ wasn't exactly ideal. Russ was pretty nearly the perfect textbook husband and father, but there had never been any real excitement there. That was all right, Val had said—the gallery provided her with all the excitement she could handle. It looked like she'd been wrong.

A car honked and passed me, and I realized I was doing about thirty-five. I laughed at myself, but I wasn't amused. I turned off the highway and drove up the next northbound street inland, where traffic would be lighter and slower.

So Stone had found out about Tony and Barbara, and had gone after Valerie to make a point. Or maybe the affair had just happened out of the blue, and that was simply Tony's interpretation of the facts. No one would ever know now. It

was pretty certain the police didn't know anything about it,
and without my source of information, they probably wouldn't
for some time.

How interested was I really in cooperating with the author-
ities—with Rob, to be exact—as far as helping them dig dirt
on my friends? Not very, right this minute.

I glanced down at the speedometer again. Twenty-five, this
time. I decided I didn't belong behind the wheel, and pulled
over to the side. When I looked up I saw Tony Garza's house
right beside me.

I don't believe in coincidence. Actually, there are a lot of
things I don't believe in, but coincidence ranks high. It was
pretty obvious to me that I had come here on purpose, kind
of sneaking up on myself. David's car was nowhere in sight,
which was good; I needed to face Tony alone, to face myself,
really.

"You are always welcome in my house," Tony told me as
he held the screen door open for me. "David is in San Diego
delivering some paintings to a gallery. He should be back in
about an hour. Would you like some lemonade?"

It was almost like it had been so long ago, and I was
almost able to remember the man I had known, and forget
the horror he had become on the outside. "I'd love some,"
I told him, stepping inside. The scruffy terrier sniffed my
shoes, then took off to chase the cat, which had been trying to sneak into the kitchen. There was a hiss and a high-
pitched yelp. The dog returned to the living room, tail tucked
under.

"He never learns," Tony said, shaking his head. "Go on out
to the patio. I'll bring the lemonade." He looked pleased to
have company.

I stepped out onto a patio of red brick gone wobbly over the
years from the force of determined weeds that had eventually
found their way up through the cracks. A table was set up
under the branches of a huge pepper tree that dominated the
backyard and lent its sharp smell to the salt and iodine that
were ever-present. I took a deep breath of the air and went
back in time.

This was the place where we would sit on warm afternoons,
Val and David and I, while Tony looked at my drawings and

spoke to us of his life before coming to California. He spoke very little at these times of his life since, and then only in generalities.

He would paint on the patio on nice days, and in a little studio he had converted from a dining room—the only room in the little house with a good north light—when the weather interfered. Later, he would build a freestanding studio building out behind the house. Now that building was a blackened patch on the earth, beginning to grow over with the green persistence of nature.

The cat pushed open a pet door and strolled out onto the patio. A mockingbird buzzed him, but he pretended not to notice.

From the kitchen I heard the rattle of ice cubes. Tony emerged with a tray, the same handpainted one he had served from when I was a girl. "Shall we sit at the table?" he asked. He added ice cubes to my glass from a bowl in the center of the tray, and poured in lemonade. "Did you bring a sketchbook for me to see?"

I laughed. It felt good. A few minutes ago I would have sworn my day, my week, my month, were totally shot. I reached into my handbag and pulled out the sketchbook I had been working in for the past month up in Cascade. Tony had a way of taking the kinks out of a person's perspective, with his acceptance, his company, and his lemonade. I was glad I had come.

It was him I saw now, more than the scars, as he leafed through the book, pausing now and then to nod at a particular sketch. "You have a good eye," he told me, pointing at a drawing of an old man I had seen from my office window, hunkering on the city sidewalk with no place in particular to go. "Have you been taking classes?"

"A few, over the years. Life drawing and anatomy, mostly."

"Those are very important. This is good work. Don't give it up." He handed back the sketchbook and I returned it to my bag. "So are you here on business or pleasure?" He refilled my glass.

"There's no real news on the case, not since yesterday."

"Well, then, I have some news for you."

"You do?"

"Don't look so surprised. I'm involved in this business, too, though I didn't want to be. Today the police came to the house, soon after David had gone. They said they were here to find evidence about the burglary. Did you know someone broke into my house? It happened about a week ago."

"Yes, I heard. Hadn't the police been here before on that matter?"

"Yes, but now they were here again. They looked around a good deal, but they left without asking me any questions about the burglary, which I thought was strange."

I thought it strange, too. "Did they look anywhere besides the house?"

"Yes. They spent almost as much time looking around the shed. There wasn't room for them and me, too, so I stayed outside."

"Was anything stolen from the shed when the house was broken into?"

"I don't think so. Some boxes were disturbed, but it's mostly just junk out there—things that have no value, but I can't seem to part with them anyway. I don't even bother to keep it locked since I'm the only one it matters to."

"Well I hope you won't have to put up with this police stuff for very much longer. Was one of the officers tall, with red hair?"

"No, I would have remembered someone like that."

I wanted to talk with him about the Keeler business, but I couldn't bear to upset him again like I had a few days before, especially without David here for him to turn to. I decided to make it a purely social call. "Well, I just came by to say hello." I took a drink. "I think I must have wanted some of this lemonade, too. Do you still make it from your own lemons?"

"That tree," he pointed to a deep green lemon tree across the yard, heavy with yellow fruit, "bears twelve months a year. I make lemonade, I make lemon pies and lemon puddings, I give lemons to my neighbors who are not so cursed with them, and still I must leave some to rot." He laughed. "I have fought a war with that tree for thirty years. Its weapons are persistence and abundance; mine are merely a knife and a juicer. When I am in the ground, that tree will drop lemons on my grave."

Tony didn't seem disturbed about the visit by the police, and I decided not to mention it further. It might mean nothing at all. How could they know there was dynamite in the shed, anyway? There was probably nothing to worry about.

I stayed until David came home, then I stayed a while longer, drinking lemonade under the pepper tree and laughing about the past so I didn't have to think about the future. Eventually, though, it was time to leave.

CHAPTER 21

· · · · · · · · · · · · · · ·

I DROVE UP IRENE'S DRIVEWAY, NOT CERTAIN IF I WANTED to see Valerie's car there or not. It wasn't there. Good. I still didn't feel up to discussing the recent revelation about her and the late Mr. Stone, and I was pretty certain I wouldn't have been able to pretend nothing was wrong—not in front of Val, the one person in the world who knows everything about me.

I parked the car and turned off the engine. After that I sat in the car and stared at Irene's landscaping, heavy on the palm trees, while time passed. Up until a couple of hours ago, I'd been pretty sure I knew everything there was to know about Val, too.

Finally, I got out of the car and trudged to the door. All things being equal, for someone who was still a huge walking bruise, I had left this place feeling pretty good a few hours before, and now I felt like a limp rag. There was a lot I still wanted to do today, but my body and mind were demanding a rest. I would sit out on the beach with a glass of iced tea, I decided, and I'd watch about ten thousand waves follow one another into shore, and I wouldn't think about anything that would cause me pain.

A car pulled up in the driveway. I turned around to see the sleek silhouette of Rob's Porsche, blinding white in the afternoon sun. I felt a moment of irritation, seeing him here now, but I strangled it and smiled.

"Hi, babe." He turned off the car and walked up to meet me on the porch with a kiss.

How could I feel bad about that? "Hi. What brings you to this neck of the beach?"

"Well, actually, I just happened to be in the neighborhood . . ."

"Right. Come in and have some iced tea. I was just going to go down to the beach."

"Sounds great."

We walked into the quiet house together. Rob looked around at the huge front room and the rich furnishings. "This is quite a setup, isn't it?"

"I always thought so. Not exactly my style anymore, though." Through the windows, I could see a huge jar of sun tea that someone, probably Valerie, had put out on the deck railing that morning. I walked out and retrieved it.

Rob joined me in the kitchen. "So what is your style, exactly?" He leaned up against a cabinet, exuding confident masculinity.

"Well, it changes." I got out glasses and ice. "When I was seventeen, I wanted a place just like this one, or just like Brian and Barbara McCain's house, which wasn't quite as grand, but really nice." I poured two glasses of tea and handed one to Rob.

We walked out onto the deck. Irene's private ocean looked as magnificent as ever. "I wanted always to live where I could see the ocean—I think I might have been a little naive about real estate values. I wanted a big, elegant house with lots of elegant furniture. I wanted to eat out every night of the week." I sighed just a bit, involuntarily. "Somewhere in there, I wanted a family, too." I started down the first flight of steps. He followed.

"And now?" he asked. "How is it different now?"

"Oh, I guess I've pulled in my expectations a bit. I live three hours from the ocean, and I almost never go there. I've got a studio apartment downtown, two blocks from my office. It's not elegant, and I seldom notice. I do go out a lot, though—mainly because I hate to cook for myself. I'm past thirty, and chances are I'll never get around to the family part."

"How would you like to have another stab at it?" he asked.

"I don't think I understand the question."

"If you could have all the things you wanted then, here and now—the house, the money, the life . . . the family—would you still want it?"

I gave it some thought, trying to treat the question seriously, though it wasn't easy. "It would be hard to turn down, I guess."

"Then don't."

"I beg your pardon?"

"I mentioned the other day that when my parents died, they left me some money. I didn't know what I wanted to do with it, so I invested it here and there, and I've made quite a bit out of it. Well, actually, it was quite a bit to begin with."

"Go on." I was beginning to get his drift, and my heart skipped a couple of beats.

"I don't want you to go back up north when this case is through. I want you to stay here. With me."

The words "this is so sudden" flitted through my mind, but I closed my mouth before they could make an exit. This was more than just an attractive offer from a handsome, sexy man I might still be in love with; it was healing for a heart broken many years before. It was the possible realization of a dream I had only recently begun to admit I'd been entertaining. It felt good.

On the other hand, it *was* sudden. I knew Rob and I had something cooking here, at the very least an ancient romance made new by constant sexual frustration—at the most, maybe a chance at a real commitment. It was the commitment part that had me speechless now.

"I guess I thought we were going to see what happened after the case was over," I managed, finally. "We've never had a real chance to explore this, as much as we might have wanted to."

"You've been in town almost a week. When this case is wrapped, you'll have to go back up north and go back to work for Jack."

"Jake."

"Whoever. What I'm trying to say is, we won't have a chance to explore anything, the way we're going. But if you were to quit your job and stay down here . . ."

"Rob, I can't quit my job."

"Why the hell not? Shit, I might quit *my* job. What I'm trying to tell you is that I can give you the kind of life you always wanted and couldn't have. I want to do that for you. I want to do everything for you."

I remained silent for what seemed like a hell of a long time, looking at his face. His eyes were burning into me. "You've got to give me some time to think about it. I mean, I've been building a career for myself the past three years. I never thought about having to quit."

"It's just a job. You said that to me once—'It's just a job.' " He moved closer, put a hand on my arm. "Caley, I love you."

There they were, the very words. How long had I been waiting to hear him say them? Traditionally, one echoes them back.

"Please. Just give me time to think."

"How long?"

"I don't know. All I know is I can't give it any consideration until all this business with Tony has been settled. I have so goddamned much on my mind right now, and frankly, I'm a little scared by all this."

He considered this for a moment. "All right. I'm sorry, I didn't mean to frighten you. When you're sure, you'll let me know." His eyes were distracted when he said this, as though he were thinking something completely different.

I could imagine the strain this confession of love had put on the facade of cool that Rob had carried around like luggage as long as I'd known him. "I will let you know. You'll know as soon as I do. And thank you, Rob—for caring, for everything."

"I do care; don't ever forget that. Still want to take a walk on the beach?"

"Sure." I finished my tea and set the glass down on the railing. We went down the steps to the last level and onto the beach, utterly devoid of any other human presence. We began to walk, not hurrying.

"So are you taking up surfing?"

"What kind of silly question is that? I don't even swim."

"I thought I saw your car in front of Andy McCain's surf shop earlier."

"Andy and I are old friends."

"By my reckoning, Andy was about ten years old when you left town last time. How much of a friend could he be?"

I could feel a frown coming on. It pulled at my stitches. "I was friends with the whole family. I've really enjoyed getting to know Andy better the last few days, and I don't think I like your tone of voice."

"Sorry. I'm taking my work on a pleasure call. This whole murder spree thing has got me on edge."

"Keeler?"

"And Stone. The newspaper and TV guys are practically camping out on my doorstep to be on the ground floor for the next murder."

"I don't suppose," I said, taking the plunge, "that you'd consider telling me anything new that's come up on the Keeler case. I don't mean anything top secret, of course."

"Somebody planted a dynamite charge on his boat. It blew up. He's dead."

"Give me a break, Sergeant. I could get more than that from the newspapers."

"Where do you think we get *our* information?"

"What a rip-off. Come on, tell me something I don't know."

"I wish I could. Dynamite's hard on evidence. They're putting together all the pieces they can find down in San Diego—it gives the sheriff's boys something to do—but I don't think they'll come up with much."

"Are *you* coming up with much?"

"Shit, Caley, you know I can't discuss this with you. Let's get off the subject, okay?"

"Okay." Rob was right; we were mixing business and pleasure. Enough, already. "Tell you what—let me show you one of my favorite places down here," I offered, taking his hand and leading him south of the house.

Walking was a workout in the soft, dry sand at the head of the beach. We headed seaward a few yards into the harder sand, to make the trek easier. After a couple of minutes, we took off our shoes and carried them.

The cliffs here were rocky and vertical; impossible to climb for anyone but a dedicated mountaineer, and impossibly beautiful. Here and there large rocks, like escapees, ventured out from the cliffs and made for the shoreline. We rounded one such fugitive, covered with algae on its seaward side, and headed landward. Here the cliff came out in a point, reaching for the water. As we approached the cliff, an opening appeared in it, created out of nothing by the shift in parallax.

"Hey!" Rob exclaimed.

"Yeah, isn't it great? You can't even see it from a few yards either way up or down shore. Val and I found it by accident when we were walking the beach one day, back in high school."

We put our shoes back on, and entered the narrow cave. Large rocks, buried in the sand at the cave mouth, made negotiating the entrance tricky and hard on the feet.

The cave went back into blackness, growing increasingly more narrow all the way. It had probably started out as a crack, then been widened a few grains at a time by millennia of high tides.

"Val was grounded," I began, stepping carefully over and between the jagged rocks. My voice echoed off the rock walls. "Irene left on one of her all-day shopping trips and Val called and asked me to come over. It was the dead of winter, so naturally we went walking on the beach."

"Naturally."

"We found this place, and decided to go exploring." We were inside the cave now, and I looked up to see a narrow splinter of sky perhaps a hundred feet above.

"How far did you get?"

"Too far. We didn't notice the tide was coming in until we were way back there, where there's barely enough room for one person to pass. We hadn't been paying any attention to the time, but when our shoes started to get wet, we made the connection."

I took Rob's hand and we walked toward the rear of the cave. The space between the walls grew narrower. "By the time we got to where we could walk two abreast, the water was up to our knees. It slowed us down considerably."

"I'll bet."

"We couldn't see the rocks on the cave floor, so we kept tripping and falling down when we tried to hurry. By the time we were halfway to the cave mouth, the waves were knocking us back; the water was almost waist-high by then."

"You must have been scared shitless."

"I can't swim a stroke. Val can, but I'm not sure how much good it would have done in those circumstances anyway." Rob and I had gone far enough back to make further passage difficult. Not too many feet ahead, a careless explorer could become wedged between rocks, and trapped.

"So, you got away, obviously."

"Obviously. We clawed our way to the cave mouth and around the corner of the opening, sort of between waves, and scrambled up beyond the shoreline. We were a vision in blue lying out on the sand on a cold, gray November afternoon being grateful for our lives."

"Did you get yelled at for being a couple of idiot kids?"

"Irene never knew. We ran back to the house and changed our clothes, and lit a fire, and treated ourselves to some of her good brandy."

Well, that wasn't one hundred percent true. David had been there when we got home, and he had yelled at us for almost getting drowned. Later, we showed him the cave, and it became a favorite place for the three of us to meet away from Irene. I had a lot of happy memories of this place, but I didn't feel like I could share them with Rob; he was a little sensitive on the subject of David.

"Anyway, I really love this cave, and I wanted to share it with you."

Rob glanced at his watch. "Doesn't look like I have time to do any more exploring today—I've got business downtown."

"Okay. Let's head back then."

He left me at the top of the stairs to take the side route out of the driveway. "Promise me you'll give some thought to staying here. Or if you don't want it to be here, we can go someplace else. Anyplace at all. Just think about it, okay?"

"Yes. I'll think about it. I probably won't be able to think much about anything else."

"That's the idea."

CHAPTER 22

. . . .

ROB HAD JUST PULLED OFF WHEN I HEARD ANOTHER CAR come up into the drive. A moment later the door opened, and Russ came in. In my present state of confusion about pretty nearly everything, it was actually a relief to see him; not many people stand in my mind for uncompromising solidity and total lack of imagination like Russ Morris. I greeted him with a smile and offered him a glass of tea, which he accepted gratefully.

"It's getting to be summer out there," he said, draining the first glass and pouring himself a refill. "Although I'll admit I'm spoiled, living close to the ocean like this all my life. I guess you inlanders really know what heat's about, huh?"

"Yeah. It can be pretty miserable in Cascade in the summer. A river runs through town, but I don't think it cools things down much unless you live right on it, and I can't afford to." I was kind of enjoying this mindless conversation; so many of my conversations with other people were hopelessly pointed, especially as they related to a case in progress.

Russ led the way into the dining room and sat down at the polished pecan table. I joined him.

"So does your mother usually pick the kids up from school? I haven't seen much of them since I've been here."

"Yeah, they go over to her place after school as often as not; sometimes they spend the night. Val and I both work late a lot.

139

We try to make up for it on the weekends—of course if Val doesn't have someone really good to take over for her at the gallery, she can't afford to be gone on summer weekends."

"It must be difficult sometimes, having two such different careers." And two such different personalities, I thought, but it didn't need to be mentioned.

He took two sterling and crystal coasters from a stack in the center of the table and passed one to me.

"Yes, it can be. Of course you know as well as anyone, I know nothing about art and care less. I tried to become interested, back in the early years—I thought maybe it was something I just hadn't been exposed to, so I tried exposing myself, if you'll pardon the terminology." He laughed at his joke and so did I—it wasn't that bad, for Russ.

"Eventually, though, it became obvious to both of us that our interests lay in different areas."

About as different as Hong Kong and Kearney, Nebraska, I thought. "But you've got your marriage, and the kids, and a lot of shared experience. That counts for a lot." I wasn't sure if I was talking to him or myself. I decided it didn't matter.

"I think we've come to a pretty good place," he said, then looked down at the table, seeming a bit shaken suddenly. "Or I thought we had," he added, very low.

I didn't know how to respond, so I didn't.

He looked back up, in control again. "So, wasn't that Rob Cameron I saw driving away a minute ago? You guys getting back together after all these years?"

"Kind of looks like it. It also looks like I'm going to have to make some life decisions here pretty soon."

"Has he proposed, or is that old-fashioned, now?"

"I think that's what he's doing. And I think it's what I want, but—I wish he wouldn't push me just now."

Russ twirled his tea glass slowly around and around on its coaster. The ice cubes clinked gently. "I can remember as clearly as if it were yesterday the day I decided I was going to marry Valerie. She wasn't sure it was what she wanted at first, but I persisted. Now I wonder if I should have pushed her so hard."

He looked at me, and I guess he could see the look that crossed my face when he mentioned Val, because he nodded, and his eyes brightened just a bit with unshed tears. "Yes, I'm worried about her, too. She's been through a lot the past week."

He took off his glasses, and polished them on a spotless white handkerchief. "I don't know how much Val confides in you, but I suspect it's quite a bit. That's good, I think. She needs a friend."

I noticed his hands trembling as he rubbed at nonexistent spots on the glasses. I felt terribly sorry for him, somehow, though I didn't know why. I was about to find out.

"I've known for more than a month that Val was having an affair with Chandler Stone." He attempted a smile, shrugged. "I guess I can't blame her, really. They say people don't usually have affairs for sex, per se, as much as for someone to communicate with. Val and I don't communicate much."

I felt like I had to offer him something to fill up the great emptiness I could see behind his eyes. "Val loves you, Russ. You've got to believe that."

"Oh, yes, I know." The smile was a little more solid this time. He ran a long-fingered hand through his pale hair. "When I realized what was happening, I thought I was going to lose her. I went a little insane there for a while, and what was *really* insane was that when I was with her, I had to pretend nothing was wrong."

"That must have been pretty awful."

"I don't know which was more terrible—the strain of keeping up the pretense, or the fear that she'd go away from me. Either way, it's over now."

It certainly was, and so was Chandler Stone. Job or no job, though, I was getting a little tired of uncovering people close to me who might have wanted him dead enough to have helped him along. With an inward sigh, I added Russ to my mental list, but I felt a definite lack of objectivity. Was he trying to confess something to me, or was he only unburdening himself to someone he perceived as a sympathetic listener?

And was I sympathetic? I certainly felt sympathy, but there was also the feeling that if I were married to Russ Morris, I might start looking elsewhere for input, too.

Russ went on. "Val took pains to keep me from knowing— I know that. She didn't do this to hurt me."

"I'm sure she didn't. Val is one of the kindest people I know." But kindness, I reminded myself, is for strangers, not lovers. "I don't mean to pry, and you don't have to answer if you'd rather not, but how did you find out?"

He raised his glass to gesture at our surroundings, and the person of whose presence we were always mindful here. "It was a gesture of purest concern on Irene's part. She couldn't bear my blissful ignorance of the facts, so she enlightened me."

"Jesus. What a stone-cold bitch. For a while I thought *she* was the one who was sleeping with Stone."

"She would have liked to. Tried, as a matter of fact, but was turned down cold. Irene's not used to losing; she didn't take it well. When she found out about Stone and Val, I think maybe it drove her a little crazy, too."

"I don't think it would take a drive—I think a short putt would do the trick."

Russ smiled at that. He'd had thirteen years of Irene, and knew her even better than I did.

"I don't ever want Val to know that she wasn't successful in saving my feelings. Promise me you'll never tell her I know."

I shook my head, adding another secret to the stack of secrets I carried with me everywhere I went. "She'll never find out from me, Russ. I love her, too."

CHAPTER 23

. . . .

I DIDN'T THINK I COULD BEAR HANGING AROUND THE HOUSE with Russ the rest of the afternoon. I excused myself as soon as possible and drove out again, south this time. It didn't seem like I ought to put off seeing Barbara Stone any longer, but I couldn't say I was looking forward to it. I decided not to call ahead, on the basis that it would be easier to turn me away on the phone than at the door. I drove up to the pink stucco gate and had a frustrating conversation with the little box on a stick before Elena finally keyed the gate open from the security console in the kitchen.

She huffed and fussed as she let me in the back door and led me into the library where I waited about ten minutes for the widow Stone to make her appearance.

Barbara was sober, or nearly, this time. Her face, without the drugged puffiness it had shown on my last visit, was almost as lovely as I remembered it from fifteen years ago. Her pale blond hair was pulled back from her face into a cluster of soft curls at the back of her head. Her bruises, faded since my last visit, looked less extreme under an artfully applied layer of makeup. She wore black stunningly, as I might have guessed— long sleeves, a high neckline, and a double strand of genuine pearls.

"Caley," she said, walking into the room with some of the old assurance that had been missing on my last visit. "My dear,

143

what happened to you?" She came closer to look at my face which was still looking pretty battered. "Have you been in an accident?"

"Yes, a couple of days ago. I'm much better now."

"I'm glad. And I'm glad you came back. I treated you dreadfully the other day." She took my hand in hers. "I hope you can appreciate what I was going through."

I could, I supposed, as well as I possibly could without having experienced the violent death of a loved one. She was being very gracious, almost too polite, and I was still feeling cautious.

"I'm sorry I had to come on business that upset you. I hope you understand that this isn't strictly a social call either."

"You have to do your job. Let's not let that make us enemies."

"I hope it doesn't have to."

"Then let's have some tea." She signaled Elena, who was lurking in a doorway with the same perpetual frown as before, and spoke to her in Spanish so terrible I could almost understand it. "Why don't we go out on the veranda? It's quite warm in here, isn't it? If we're lucky, the onshore breeze should be getting under way."

She led the way out a set of double glass doors to a tiled and half-walled veranda roughly twice the size of my entire apartment. A white-painted wrought-iron table and chairs occupied the center of it, with assorted chaises for lounging, and a multitude of immense clay pots planted with brilliant annuals of the season. A solemn gray Persian perched on the pink stucco wall and watched us approach. Barbara reached out to pet him, which he tolerated with some grace.

"I imagine you've heard about Leo Keeler."

"Yes. It was dreadful. Of course he was a dreadful man; still, what an awful way to die. It's been all over the television and newspapers, you know, two murders in five days."

"Yes, I've seen some articles in the San Diego papers— 'Murder Beach,' and all that. Pretty lurid stuff. Did Mr. Stone know Leo Keeler at all, do you know?"

"Chandler know Leo? No, I'm certain he didn't. He knew *of* him, to be sure. It would be difficult to live in this town and never have heard of Leo. He was a presence of sorts, not a particularly benign one, but a presence."

"And you can't think of any reason they would have known each other, done business together, or perhaps had mutual business associates?"

She laughed. "No, I'm afraid I can't. I'm sorry, I don't mean to hurt your feelings, Caley, but it is a pretty ridiculous thought, isn't it?"

I laughed, too, but I didn't feel it. "Yes. Ridiculous. You understand I have to try to think of everything, cover all bases . . ."

"Of course you do. It must be awfully exciting to do what you do. Never a dull moment."

"Oh, lots of dull moments, actually. There's usually more boredom than danger in the investigation business."

"Still, you're out there, doing something in the real world. I haven't done anything worth talking about since I gave up my law practice."

And your husband, I added mentally, but what did I know? Maybe life with Brian had been as painfully boring for Barbara as life with Russ was for Val. Boredom had not been the watchword of my marriage, so I couldn't say what I would have done in either of their positions.

Elena came with silver tea things on a silver tray, and began laying them out on the white tablecloth. A breeze came by and stirred the white linen napkins. I remembered how I used to feel coming to Barbara McCain's house from my family's rather modest two-bedroom place; much the same as I felt at Irene Hayden's—as though I had walked into the world behind the movie screen.

Barbara had never seemed to notice anything out of the ordinary about her life; she had been born to live this way. Her parents still rattled around in one of those pink Spanish palaces you see crowding the hills above Laguna. She had been driven to school in a Rolls—private school, of course. To her, living like this was simply the norm.

Frequently, when I had lived in Morado Beach before, Barbara and Brian would go away overnight, leaving me with Andy. I would walk around touching the furniture and dishes and the silver tea service on the sideboard, imagining that I might live like that someday.

Someday had come and gone, and I lived in a one-room apartment over a decorator's studio across from a bookstore. I liked my life, I was fond of saying; I had said so to Rob, the night of the reunion. Now Rob was promising me something I didn't know how to handle: the life I'd always said I wanted. I wrenched myself back into the present with an effort.

When Elena had gone back inside, I took a deep breath and asked a touchy question. "As far as you know, was Mr. Stone ever unfaithful to you?"

Barbara poured a cup of amber tea into a translucent white teacup and placed it in front of me. "Well, he didn't come home and talk about it, but knowing him, I'd be very surprised if he didn't have at least one woman on the side—maybe several. Chandler wasn't the kind of man who could be satisfied with one woman."

I raised an eyebrow. "I'm surprised you can talk about it so calmly."

"I'm a grown-up." She smiled briefly and coolly. "I think I have a pretty good grasp on how things work in the real world. Chandler was . . . how shall I put it? Larger than life. He was a man of enormous passions, and everything was a passion to him. Women were only a part of the picture, but I'm certain he didn't neglect them." She poured tea for herself.

This visit was certainly going better than the last one, I noted. Barbara had answered a couple of questions, and I wasn't out on my ear yet. Well, before I started congratulating myself, I had more questions to ask. I went through a quick mental list of knowns and unknowns, and came up with a couple:

"How long had Mr. Stone known Edmund Berenson?"

"He came to town about a year after Chandler did. They'd known each other for some time by then. I think they'd done business in Los Angeles some years back. Chandler sent for him to handle certain financial aspects of the business; Ed's a wizard with investments, you know."

"That's what I keep hearing." I watched her face, matched it with her voice, mannerisms, and choice of words. From all I could tell, she really didn't know what I knew about Berenson.

We drank our tea and watched the sun get lower over the

Pacific. It was restful and almost friendly, in a cautious sort of way. Barbara was different now, more guarded, more formal. It was okay, though. I could recognize an imbedded defense mechanism—I had a few of my own.

"The police haven't been around since before the weekend," she said after a few minutes of companionable silence. "Do you know if there have been any further developments in the case?"

"They're still not certain who killed Mr. Stone," I said, watching her face, "but they think it might have been Antonio Garza."

"Oh, no." Her eyes widened as she looked at me. "Surely they can't think it was Tony. Why would Tony have wanted to kill Chandler?"

"Did the police ask you that question?"

She thought about this for a moment. Obviously the police had been around when she was drugged out of her mind, like I had; she was having some difficulty recalling the interview. "I don't think so. I'm sure I would have remembered that. They did want to know if I could think of anyone who might have hated Chandler. Just a general sort of question—they didn't mention any names."

"Were you able to come up with anyone?"

"I think a man doesn't get to be in Chandler's place in the world without making some enemies, but they're enemies of a different kind. As for people who may have wished him dead"—a shadow passed behind her eyes and was gone—"I couldn't give them any names."

Not exactly the same thing as not *knowing* any names, I noted. Whose name was she keeping to herself? Brian's? Andy's? Her own?

"And you don't think Tony would have done it?"

"I've known Tony Garza for more than twenty years. Since Brian and I first came to Morado Beach, when Andy was just a baby." She gazed off, remembering. "I've been buying his art for almost that long. I have one of the most extensive Garza collections in the state."

She looked back at me. "Would he be capable of killing? He's a man of very strong feelings; I think he might do nearly anything to protect someone he loved. Perhaps he could kill if it were a matter of something like that. But why Chandler? They barely knew each other."

"Edmund Berenson says he heard the tail end of an argument between Tony and Mr. Stone three days before the shooting, and that it was about a woman."

Barbara's hand went involuntarily to the base of her throat. "Did he . . . did anyone hear a name mentioned?" Her face had gone quite pale under the makeup, and the bruise showed, yellow and faded. Almost, it made her look her age.

I could guess what she was probably thinking, but I didn't know if I wanted to spill everything I knew about her and Tony, and there was no reason yet to say anything about Val. I decided to play dumb; I do it so well. "He didn't hear a name—he came in on the tail end of it—but the argument was very bitter. The police are using it in their case to prove Tony had intent to kill your husband."

"But that's terrible. No, I can't believe it."

"I don't believe it either. That's why I'm trying to clear Tony. Have you seen him since he came home from the hospital?"

"Once. I couldn't make myself go back again."

I nodded. It was understandable of course, but I wondered how many old lovers and friends had dropped out of Tony's life since the accident. I was glad I hadn't ended up being one of them.

A breeze wafted onto the veranda, cooling me considerably. I looked at Barbara in her long-sleeved dress. "You must be terribly warm in that. I hope you didn't think you had to dress up for me."

Barbara touched her arm. "Oh, no . . . it's the medication. I'm always a little cold now. Actually, I'm quite comfortable in this."

She was quite comfortable now, but when I had first come in, she'd been too warm. Were the long sleeves hiding something? I searched the bruise on her face, and remembered it as I had seen it on the day of my first visit.

She claimed it had happened that day, but I had some recent personal experience with the lovely color scheme of bruised flesh. Right now David's bruises and mine were just beginning to fade past their original angry purple-red, and we were a

ouple of days past acquiring them. The marks on Barbara's
ace had been tinged with green, adding a couple more days
> their apparent age. That meant that whatever happened
> Barbara could have happened while Chandler Stone was
:ill alive.

Andy hadn't mentioned it, maybe he didn't even know, but
ae kind of dependency relationship that apparently existed
etween Barbara and Chandler Stone frequently includes
hysical abuse, and abusing his wife didn't seem to be an
:t that would be beneath the Chandler Stone I was coming
> know.

"He hit you, didn't he? Chandler, I mean. He made that
ruise on your face, didn't he?" The question must have come
ompletely out of left field, from Barbara's point of view, but
was hoping to shock her into an honest reply.

For half a second she seemed to be trying to summon an
ngry defense. Then her shoulders slumped and the starch
eemed to go out of her. After a moment of silence she
odded.

"But you haven't said anything to the police about it."

"No. But not for the reason you're probably thinking. I'm
ot the one who killed Chandler, though there were times I
/anted to." She blinked, and a tear escaped down her cheek.
I didn't tell them because I didn't want to be humiliated."

"But they must have seen your face. Didn't they ask you
bout it?"

"Yes. I lied to them, like I lied to you. I've been lying about
ruises, and wearing clothes like this"—she held up her arms,
lad to the wrist in black knit fabric—"for more than six years.
Ie almost never hit me on the face, you know. Only when he
vas very, very angry. It wouldn't do for Mrs. Chandler Stone
o entertain clients with a black eye, now would it?" A bitter
alf smile came and went on her face.

I felt, not for the first time, as though doing my job on this
:ase was causing me to dig too deeply into the secret lives of
>eople I cared about. "I'm so sorry" was all I could manage
>y way of an apology.

"No, *I'm* sorry. I've been in a drugged-out haze for seven
rears. Your visit the other day helped show me how low I've
unk. This time next week I'll be checking into a clinic in San

Clemente. So you see, Chandler's death had some benefici&
side effects."

Beneficial for Barbara, and certainly for Valerie in the lon&
run, but there hadn't been any benefits for Tony. Even Barbar&
couldn't say he wasn't capable of killing Stone under the rig&
circumstances. I wondered if I was ever going to come up wi&
anything that would help him.

CHAPTER 24

· · · · · · · · · · · · · ·

HE LIGHT WAS FADING TO PURPLE, BUT THE GALLERY WAS
ill open. I went inside. Easel and track lighting accented doz-
ns of paintings, only slightly crowded into the large front area
here the tourists tended to come and buy. A Mozart sympho-
y—the 29th—eked out perfection in measured, eighteenth-
entury doses through the room speakers. A coffee maker
ffered hospitality. I accepted.

A nice, affluent couple, in shiny new clothes identifying
hem as upper-middle-class vacationers, were consulting with
'al on some seascapes. To my eye, they were close enough to
lentical as not to matter, but these folks were filling up a big
hunk of wall a thousand miles from any real ocean, and to
hem it mattered. I walked past, raising a hand to Val to let her
now I was there, and went down into the next room, where
could see Garza landscapes brightening one wall.

I had never been to New Mexico, except in Tony's paint-
ngs, but I felt like I knew it. He would tell Val and David
nd me stories of his boyhood while he painted those spare and
ubtle landscapes populated with the people he had left behind
ong ago.

I stood in front of a painting of sheep being herded through
canyon by two girls in brilliant skirts. The sky took up fully
wo thirds of it, with clouds piling up on the canyon rim. I
ould feel the weight of those clouds, that sky.

"Tony used to say that the sky was more important i
New Mexico than anywhere else he'd ever been." I turne
at the sound of the voice and saw David leaning again:
the doorjamb, arms crossed in front of his chest. He cam
up and stood beside me and we took in that vast bluenes
together.

"I'd love to see it sometime for myself."

"Tony took me there once, years ago. It's very much lik
that, and like Tony's other paintings. Seeing it gave me
better understanding of him. Oh, by the way, I have somethin
for you."

"Something important?"

"Vitally." He reached into his shirt pocket and withdrew
small box. "Sorry it's not wrapped." He handed it to me.

"Thank you. What's the occasion?"

"You'll understand when you open it. Go on."

"Okay, here goes." I lifted the lid from the box to fin
another box with a hinged lid. I opened that one to revea
a brand-new Mickey Mouse watch—a replacement for mine
which was lying in pieces at the bottom of a hospital personal
effects envelope.

"David, I don't know what to say."

"How about 'You shouldn't have'?"

"Well, you shouldn't, but I'm glad you did. I've been los
without Mickey. Thank you." I reached up and kissed hi
cheek, then turned around and started putting on the watc
to cover my own consternation. He said nothing, but I coul
feel his presence behind me like the heat of an open fire.

I looked around the room. "So where's your stuff? No, don'
tell me, I can find it."

Across the room were half a dozen portraits and othe
people-heavy pieces. Where Tony's people served to ancho
his landscapes in the real world, David's people were th
reason, the question, the answer to every piece. Their person
alities flowed, burst, sometimes burned out of the canvases
Their settings were there to emphasize them, to augment th
statements they made by their presence on two-dimensiona
rectangles of cloth.

"Jesus, David," I said when I had my breath back. "I'm
afraid now to have you paint me."

"Afraid I can't handle it, huh?" He came up and put a hand on my shoulder.

I turned to face him. "No, afraid you'll get my soul onto canvas the way you did these people, and I won't like what I see."

"I like what I see. Trust me." He pulled me closer to him. The fear must have shown on my face, because he let go again, touched my hair, smiled. "I don't mean to get closer than you want me to. I'm sorry."

"Don't be," I said, but my voice wasn't working too well. "I just don't know what I want right now. I don't know what's important."

"Friendship is important. Don't run off again, Caley. Even if you get your heart broken again, don't run off like you did before."

"I won't. I promise." I looked up to see Val in the doorway. She was smiling at the sight of what she imagined to be a romantic moment between David and me. Well, maybe it was. I knew David cared about me in ways that went beyond friendship, or maybe just existed beside it. I wished I felt free to examine my own feelings on the matter, but I didn't. Whenever I tried, I shied away inside. Why couldn't life be simple?

I smiled back at Val and walked over to meet her halfway. "Friendship is important," David had said. How right he was.

"Berenson," I said, going down a very short list. "Andy McCain. Brian McCain. Unnamed bad guys from L.A."

"Barbara Stone," David added. He poured the last few ounces of a beer into his glass. We had finished a huge dinner, and were sitting in Garcia's at one of those ridiculous little cocktail tables designed for playing kneesies under. Fortunately or otherwise, Val was sitting between us.

"Yes, she's on here, too."

"What would her motive be?" Val asked.

"Well, motive isn't important by itself. If a person has one, and if they've shown in some way that they intended to commit the crime, and if they could have been at the right place at the right time, and can't prove they weren't, then things start getting sticky. If evidence is found linking them to the crime scene, the case gets stronger. Alibis are dandy, but guilty people usually have one, too."

"Well, what's Barbara's story anyhow?"

"Just that Stone seems to have gone out of his way to get her strung out on cocaine and a few other things. She was dependent on him for her supply. That kind of dependency can work against you if a person gets desperate. And Barbara could have been desperate. Stone had been physically abusing her almost as long as they'd been married." I looked at Val to see how she would take this statement—she seemed troubled by it, as I might have expected. I went on. "Barbara could conceivably have driven to town and back from Costa Azul without being missed by Elena, and the gardener was out of town."

"Maybe Stone was playing house with the maid, and she killed him out of jealousy," David suggested as he pushed away from the table. "Excuse me, ladies—I have to make a pit stop."

Val's eyes followed David, wounded. I put my hand on hers. "Hey, it's okay. He doesn't know."

She turned to me slowly, eyes wide. "But you do." It wasn't a question.

I nodded.

"You must be terribly disappointed in me." Her eyes gleamed with tears.

"At first. It would have been useful for me to know the whole story at the beginning. Then I took some time to think about it. You're the only one who can decide what to tell someone else and what to keep to yourself. You're also the only one who knows what's best for your life."

She shook her head, eyes closed. "Chandler wasn't best. Not by a long shot. What's killing me is that Tony knew. What must he think of me?"

"Tony loves you, Val. He's not judging you."

"I guess you're right. It's just that I've let so many people down."

"Mostly yourself. I think it's time to go forward, now."

"You don't think Russ knows . . ."

"No," I lied, and it was so easy, so incredibly easy, this healing lie. "Russ doesn't know."

A tension went out of her body. "You have no idea what a relief this is, not having to pretend around you anymore. We'll talk about it, I promise."

"I know. When all this is over." So many things were going to happen when all this was over.

David came back to the table. "Shall we order another round?"

"Might as well," I said, swishing the last drops around in the bottom of my beer bottle. "We're not getting anywhere sober."

He waved at the waitress, pointed to our empties. "So go on with the list."

"Well, that's about it right now," I said. "Berenson definitely stood to profit—a quarter of a million worth. The exercise bunny could be stretching the truth about when he was at her place, and it's only a few blocks from Stone and Berenson's office.

"As for hardasses from the big city, they'd have come in and done the job and gotten out clean. That's still a possibility, of course. The gun still hasn't turned up. It could be on the ocean floor fifty miles north of here."

"Brian McCain?"

"Brian doesn't feel like a strong possibility to me. He wasn't that far from the scene, and his assistant might be willing to lie for him, but I think if he were going to kill Stone for stealing his wife, it would have happened years ago. He's not the kind of guy who hangs on to a grudge. He's still on the list, though. He's been out of town since Friday afternoon. Of course guilt is not the only reason people leave town. In this case, it's his aging mother."

"And Andy?"

"Nope. Andy didn't kill anybody."

"What's your reasoning?"

"Less professional reason; I just don't think he did it. Of course he's also covered for the time of the murder."

It seemed silly to say "he told me he didn't do it." Wouldn't anyone? But I had been there when he said it, and I had seen his eyes—some part of him regretted not having killed Stone. That was more believable than anyone's denial.

The waitress replaced our empties with frosty bottles of dark ale. I like a beer that stands up and fights back; I took a long drink of mine.

"Who doesn't have an alibi?" David asked.

I sighed. "Everybody in California has an alibi for that night except your grandfather. Of course, any alibi could be a lie, too."

"So assuming that any alibi could be a lie, I could have done it."

"Any of a thousand people might have done it, but only someone with a reason *would* have. All these people had possible reasons to do Stone in—what's your motive?"

"I guess I don't have one. I didn't like him, particularly, but I never bumped into him that much. Val knew him better than I did." And Val, being emotionally entangled, was a more likely suspect as well, I reminded myself. I wondered for the hundredth time in five days what I was doing working on a case for my best friend. I wasn't objective, and it wasn't good for my mental health.

"I don't know," I mused. "I keep coming back to Berenson. I know his gun hadn't been fired, but you can get a gun anywhere if you know who to ask. You can even get someone to pull the trigger for you. Murder for financial gain may not be as common as the good old crime of passion, but I can't rule it out, no matter how obvious it seems. It's money he needed real bad."

I took another drink of my beer. "The fun part comes in trying to connect Stone and Keeler, using any interface besides Tony. If Keeler really had been running drugs into town, that would have been one possibility. As it is, Rob seems to think Tony's the best suspect he's got."

David shot me a look.

I felt awful. I hadn't intended to bring Rob into this discussion, and especially like that. "Yeah, I know, 'Fuck Rob.' "

"I'd rather you didn't, but that's up to you."

Valerie drummed her fingers on the table. "So. Nice weather we're having."

I laughed, and David and Val laughed with me. We all had a good laugh and another beer.

CHAPTER 25

· · · · · · · · · · · · ·

WHEN WE GOT HOME, VALERIE GAVE ME AN EXHAUSTED HUG and went up to bed. I wandered into the front room to sit for a while. The message light on the phone was blinking; I decided to see if anyone had been trying to reach me. After Russ's "working late, don't worry" message and Irene's "staying over with friends in Newport Beach" message was a breathless communication from Andy: "You're going to love this one, Ms. Detective. I've got some stuff to do at the shop, so I'll wait here for you until one or so. Hurry, though."

It was just past midnight. I raced down to Hot Surf, keeping a weather eye in the rearview mirror for the M.B.P.D. When I walked in the door, Andy was standing behind the counter holding up a piece of paper, a wicked smile on his face.

I snatched the paper out of his fingers. "What is it?" I asked, scanning it for quick information.

"A rental contract I found at my mother's."

"Andy, the guy was in the real estate business!"

"A rental contract on a warehouse in Chula Vista. Check out the signature."

"E. Bjornsen." I looked up at him, amazement clearly showing on my face.

He nodded, still smiling like a young devil. "Your friend and mine."

"How did you find this? Tell me everything."

"Sure, boss. Beer?"

"No thanks, I've done that already tonight."

"Coffee, then?"

"Absolutely." I didn't know what any of it meant yet, but it was pretty good evidence that Stone had at least known that Berenson was Bjornsen, and would tend to lend credence to the idea of an out-of-town assassin, removing Stone from the ranks of honest real estate developers and associating him more firmly with the kind of people who send out guys to push other guys' buttons for them. I was feeling pretty encouraged as I accepted a foam cup of coffee from Andy.

"Well, I went by to see Mom tonight, and she crashed early and told me to let myself out, and I did, only not right away."

"Right."

"I went upstairs to Stone's study. It was always locked before, but I think the police must have needed to look at it, and it didn't get locked back up."

Stone had been pretty neat about his paperwork, Andy said. There wasn't a lot of stuff lying about, and as luck would have it, Elena had emptied the wastebasket. About the time he became convinced he wasn't going to find anything, he had the bright idea of removing the drawers, to check for false bottoms (obviously, he had been seeing too many detective movies). It was a good move, though, because a few pieces of paper had fallen down behind one of the drawers, and stayed there. Most were of no interest, but one was a real find.

The contract described a warehouse, complete with an address in Chula Vista, a back bedroom community of San Diego, about halfway to the Mexican border from the city proper.

"Why would these guys need a warehouse more than forty miles away," Andy asked, "when they could get one right here in town that they probably already owned?"

"Why would they need one at all? Supposedly, they weren't dealing in warehousable goods."

"And why would they have to rent it under another name?"

"I wish there were some way we could find out what's in there." We looked at each other for a minute, our minds racing.

By skirting San Diego on the freeway, we could be in Chula Vista in less than an hour without speeding.

We sped anyway.

The warehouse was located in an industrial neighborhood made up of almost identical prefab metal buildings. It stood in a row of its clones, most of which were broken up into the offices of various small businesses and manufacturers. The sign above the door matching the address on the contract read "Lapierre Computer Systems."

"I knew my high school French would come in handy some day," I told Andy. "*La pierre* is French for 'stone.'"

We parked the Subaru in the dark beyond the building lights and went up to check the place out close up. There were blinds on the windows, and they were shut tight, of course. The sign was somewhat weather-worn, leading me to think it was probably a few years old. There was a smaller plastic sign on the door, declaring "Deliveries in back of building."

"Deliveries of what?" Andy quipped.

We walked around to the back, where a big sliding door was locked securely. A smaller back entrance looked less secure, as though it might even yield to a standard amateur trick like a credit card. I fumbled around in my bag for one.

Andy laid a hand on my arm. A pair of headlights rounded the corner of the building, and a spotlight shone on us from a big sedan somewhere beyond the glare.

"Excuse me, folks, can I help you?"

I went into a mental tap dance. "I don't think so. Well, maybe you can. My brother and I have been driving around looking for the name of whoever owns these buildings, or an agent at least. We want to rent one for our business." I indicated my handbag, which was still open. "I was just getting ready to leave a note on this door."

"May I see your ID, ma'am?"

I knew he didn't have the right to ask me that, but I didn't want to push it. I handed him one of two I carry for just these types of situations. "Do you work for the owners of the building? I'd be very interested to know what they're charging per square foot." I gave it all the sincerity I could muster.

He handed back the license. "Afraid not, Miss Barton. I work for Gold Star Security. They'd know the name of the owner, though. You can give them a call tomorrow. Meanwhile, this isn't exactly the best neighborhood to be wandering around in after midnight, if you know what I mean."

Did I ever. I thanked him, and we walked back to the car like a couple of respectable people minding their own business.

"You realize," I said to Andy as I started the car and turned it around, "that Lapierre Computer Systems could just possibly be a perfectly legitimate subsidiary of Stone & Berenson."

His eyebrows shot up. "Is that what you think?"

"Shit, no. You think I'm totally stupid?"

CHAPTER 26

THE NEXT MORNING IRENE WAS BACK, BUSTLING ABOUT IN the kitchen like a crazed housewife. After commenting on my battered appearance, she offered me breakfast, and I decided to take her up on it. If nothing else, I wanted to observe her in her natural habitat. Irene was not one of the people on the list I'd made for Val and David at Garcia's, but after her behavior a few nights before, she had a spot on an invisible list I kept in my head.

In my ideal outcome scenario for this mess, I didn't want the person who killed Stone—or Keeler either—to be anyone even vaguely related to any friend of mine, but fate, or whatever it is, usually seems amused by our want lists, so I never mention mine aloud for fear of being overheard.

I took some coffee and sat down in the dining room. Irene came in a few minutes later with two plates of food. "So. Are you enjoying your visit? Other than almost being blown up, that is." She smiled briefly as she unfolded a linen napkin and spread it out on her lap. I followed suit.

"Other than that, yes, I guess so. I've been doing a lot of visiting around, talking to people . . ." All true, all not nearly the truth. The truth would make the conversation stop dead.

I took a bite of cheese and mushroom omelet, and thought I'd try for some incidental information, anyway. "This is delicious."

"Thank you. Years of cooking classes have paid off."

"I've been wondering, Irene. Did you know Leo Keeler at all, other than just seeing him around town, that is?"

"Leo Keeler?" She seemed both surprised and amused. "Why on earth would you ask a question like that?"

I gave it my best offhand manner. "It's just that I've been hearing so much about him from everyone since the explosion. I don't remember all that much about him from when I lived here, but I guess he was really some kind of town character."

Irene cut into her omelet. "I don't know as I'd put it in just those terms, but he was pretty well known. My mother knew him, when he was younger."

"Really? I had no idea."

"Yes. She took me to meet him once. I think I was about seven years old at the time."

"What was he like, back then?"

"I think we were only there a few minutes. They had some sort of argument and we left soon after we arrived. All I remember is that I thought him very handsome; dark good looks—Black-Irish, I suppose. I remember his eyes were very dark and lively. He had quite a reputation with the ladies, I later found out. Of course I was too young to know what he was really like."

"By the time I remember him, he certainly wasn't handsome."

"That's what dissipation does to a person, I suspect. They say he took to drink early, and went downhill fast."

"Some people think he had nowhere to go down from."

"He had quite a few enemies, I suppose. That's what I've always heard."

"At least one, unless you subscribe to the theory that someone left a set dynamite charge on his boat by accident."

She arched an eyebrow. "I'm sure the police will catch whoever did it."

Maybe. My biggest worry right now was that they would catch someone who *didn't* do it.

I finished my breakfast and offered to do the dishes, but Irene insisted she would only put them in the dishwasher, and I should get out into the sunshine and enjoy the rest of my vacation. I wished people would stop automatically prescribing sunshine for all ailments of body and soul; all it ever caused me was sunburn.

I wanted to go and see Rob. He was going to be bowled over by the Chula Vista stuff, and with some glee I anticipated the look on his face when I showed him that contract. First, though, I decided to go by Tony's. I wasn't sure how much I would enjoy running my latest bit of info past him, but I wanted to see his reaction when I told him what Irene had just told me.

Irene always spoke of her mother as though she had been some kind of saint, but the possibility certainly occurred to me, if it hadn't to her, that her mother may have been messing around with Keeler while she was married to Tony. If Tony knew that, it could have something to do with their feud. I needed to know if what was between them was really worth killing for, even after fifty years, before I could be sure Tony hadn't killed him, and sure he was actually out of danger of being arrested for it.

I walked up to the screen door and knocked. There was no answer. I tried the door; it was locked.

"Are you a friend of Mr. Garza's?" a woman's voice asked from the other side of an overgrown hedge. I looked over to see the top of a white head, which began moving down the hedge toward the sidewalk. A tiny old woman in a flowered polyester muumuu emerged at the end, and advanced toward me, waving a garden trowel. "It's terrible! I simply couldn't believe what I was seeing!"

"What's terrible?" I asked. I was beginning to feel genuine alarm. I didn't need another complication, and neither did Tony.

"The police!" she cried, gesturing at a spot in front of the house with the trowel. "They came early this morning, while I was weeding out here in my yard. I try to keep the place looking nice, you know, and I even asked Mr. Garza if he'd consider letting me help him keep his yard up a bit more, you know since his accident . . ."

"What about the police?"

"I couldn't believe what I was seeing. It was just terrible!" She shook her head sadly, looked up at me. "They took him away!"

CHAPTER 27

· · · · · · · · · · · · · ·

I RACED TO THE GALLERY, BUT VAL HAD ALREADY HEARD from Tony and had left for the jail, leaving a bewildered clerk from the bookstore next door to field questions from two ladies in pink shorts. "It was some kind of family emergency, was all she said," he told me. "I hope she gets back soon. You wouldn't happen to know the difference between these two seascapes?"

"Sorry. If you've seen one of those things . . ."

"Yeah. I know."

The Morado Beach City Jail was a tiny affair of maybe half a dozen pastel-green cells appended to the police department. Val was already there, pacing up and down the cheerless reception area. When she saw me, she broke into tears. I went over and put an arm around her shoulders and led her to a chair. "They won't let me see him yet. I don't even know what he's being charged with. How will they treat him? He's still so weak. I don't know what to do!"

"First, calm down. You can't let Tony see you this upset. Second, where's David?"

"He went to San Diego to buy some art supplies. He won't be back until late this afternoon."

"That's okay, there's nothing he could do here but worry; I think you can take care of that department until he gets back. I'm going to go talk to Rob and try to get some information. You wait here and talk to Tony as soon as they'll let you, only don't act hysterical. He needs to feel some confidence coming from somewhere. You're it right now."

Val pulled a tissue from her purse and wiped her eyes. "Okay. I can do it."

"Good. I'll be back as soon as I can."

Rob wasn't in his office, but looking out the window from Hogan's desk, I caught sight of a tall, slender redhead in uniform khaki heading for a patrol car. I hurried outside to catch Fitzpatrick.

"Sergeant Cameron got a warrant for Mr. Garza's arrest first thing this morning, Ms. Burke," Pat said. "For the murder of Leo Keeler."

"Where is he now? I need to talk with him. I've got to have more information."

"Well, ma'am, I don't know that you're going to get it from him. He doesn't even tell me everything he knows. He didn't even take me along when he went out to make the arrest. Seems like all I get to do on this case is the scut work, and I do most of that without much information to go on. I wish the sergeant had a little more faith in me."

"What can you tell me, Pat?" I looked up at him, but he avoided my eyes.

"The problem is, Ms. Burke, I don't know what I *should* be telling you."

"Just tell me if he's got any solid physical evidence, or a witness who can put Tony at the scene. Can you do that much for me? A lot depends on it."

Pat looked down at me. "You didn't hear this from me, Ms. Burke, but I'm pretty sure it's all circumstantial up to now. Sergeant Cameron thinks there might be a break in the case in the next day or two—he's pretty mum about just what he thinks it'll be—and he wanted to get Mr. Garza into custody so he didn't take it into his head to run off."

"Run off? Jesus, Pat, he's never gone two feet from this town since Wednesday night, knowing he was the prime suspect in Chandler Stone's shooting. Keeler's been dead more than two days, and he *still* wasn't going anywhere. What the hell does he mean, 'run off'?"

"You don't have to convince me, Ms. Burke. I don't know why Sergeant Cameron felt like he had to make the arrest right now, either. He seems to think he's onto something hot though. He lit out to follow some leads as soon as Mr. Garza was in custody."

Following leads, I wondered, or avoiding me? "Speaking of leads, what do you know about the print comparisons Rob was having run on Edmund Berenson?"

"Comparison with what, ma'am?"

"With Eddie Bjornsen, the dirty money man from L.A."

Pat sighed. "I don't know anything about that, Ms. Burke. It just goes to prove what I said before: the sergeant doesn't have enough faith in me to keep me abreast of the case. I'll see what I can find out for you, though, okay?"

"Okay, Pat. And Sergeant Cameron won't hear about any of this from me. I promise." I felt bad about going behind Rob's back, but Tony's innocence was at stake and I had no choice.

I waited for Val to come out of the visitor's area. The fourth estate was still very much in evidence, but their boredom had been replaced by breathless anticipation. An arrest had been made at last, and not only that, but the arrestee was something of a celebrity in his own right. The chief of police himself had apparently promised them a statement, and they awaited his appearance with cameras and recorders at the ready.

After a few minutes Val emerged shaken but holding together. I led her outside before the mob could get the idea she might be connected to the case.

"I've called Brian McCain," she said. "He got back into town this morning. He said something about a habeas corpus. Doesn't that mean something about a body?"

"A body of evidence. They can't hold Tony more than three days without showing evidence that he killed Leo. At least enough to bind him over for trial. Personally, I think Rob is going to use that time to come up with something that will enable him to charge Tony with Stone's killing, too."

"What kind of evidence? What could he possibly have?"

"I wish I knew. I'm going to talk to Tony now, and I may have to ask him some questions he doesn't want to answer. I hope he understands what's at stake." Actually, I had no doubt Tony understood perfectly what was at stake. My fear was that he simply didn't care.

wasn't easy, seeing him seated on the other side of a
eavy wire mesh, his spotless white shirt traded in for faded
lue denim. Unlike Val, I knew some of the indignities he had
uffered to get this far in the process. I felt it was partly my
ault he was here in the first place, and I wished there were
ome way I could help without having to cause him pain or
natter the secrets he'd been guarding so carefully. But at least
 could hope that in the end I would have helped more than I
rould have hurt.

Tony looked up, and almost smiled. "Hello, *niña*. I'm afraid
 have no lemonade to offer you."

"We'll have a glass together soon," I told him, "on your
atio. Right now we need to talk about Leo Keeler."

"Leo, yes. The man has been a trial to me for fifty years,
nd now that he is dead, he is even more of a trial. The police
ow have another reason to think me a murderer."

"Brian McCain is going to file a writ of habeas corpus.
'ou'll be out of here in a few days. I'm going to do everything
 can to help, but I need help from you, too."

"I'm sure I've been too rude to mention it, but I'm glad you
re doing this unpleasant job for us."

"I'm glad I was here to do it. I didn't want the job at first."

"I know. You did it for friendship, and I have not been
eating you as a friend should. My lack of concern was
artly an act I put on for Valerie and David. It's true I was
ot terribly worried when Chandler Stone was murdered. He
as my enemy, but a man like that must have many enemies.
le laughed when I threatened his life—did you know that?"

"Yes."

"He laughed when I told him I knew what he had done. . . ."
le trailed off, watching me for any reaction.

"I know what he did. I know why you said those things
 him."

Tony nodded. "Men like that know nothing of love, only of
aining advantage over another, even their lovers. Leo Keeler
vas such a man, too. And he was my enemy by his own choice,
nd now he is dead, too. It's as though I could strike down my
nemies without lifting a hand. I did not kill those men. At one
me or another, I wanted to kill both of them, but I did not.

When I see a spider in my kitchen sink, I open the window
and put her outside." He chuckled at this seeming incongruity.
"I know it is possible for a man to be convicted of a crime he
did not commit." He looked around at his surroundings. "Just
now that possibility seems quite real to me. I have no proof
of where I was when they died. And there are other things."

Other things—like dynamite. "Will you speak to me now?"

"Yes. Ask what you must ask."

Finally, a light at the end. A deep breath was in order. "Did
you know that your wife knew Leo Keeler when you were
married?"

"She also knew him before we were married. Where did
this information come from?"

"Irene told me her mother took her to see Keeler once when
she was about seven years old. They argued."

He sat there for perhaps a full minute, gathering his thoughts.
"My wife—her name was Linda—left me around that same
time, when Irene was seven. She did not come home one night
and she did not come home ever again. I received a letter from
Sacramento some weeks later, then nothing more. She left me
a daughter who already hated me. I raised her as best I could,
but I couldn't make her love me." His gaze turned upward as
he recalled images from his past. I waited for more to come
on its own.

"Linda is Spanish for 'beautiful,' and my wife was very
beautiful, but she was not Mexican. Her Anglo family dis-
owned her when we married. I was not the son-in-law they
wanted, but neither was Leo Keeler."

I met his eyes. There was a story there, one that had lain hid-
den for fifty years. I knew I was about to be the first to hear it.

He regarded me from eyes full of memories and pain. "You
deal very often in other people's secrets, don't you, *niña*?"

"Yes, I do. Sometimes I feel buried under the weight of
them." David, Val, Russ, a hundred others. I felt like I was
carrying parts of them around with me.

"I thought so. And I think also that a secret would be
safe with you. What I'm about to tell you has the power
to hurt people we both love. I can't keep you from telling
it—I can only ask you to consider what it would cost if
you did."

"I think I understand."

"When I married my wife she was sixteen years old. I was eighteen. It was different then. This was fifty-three years ago, almost another world. In those days, young women were expected to act in a certain way, but Linda was like a young animal—wild and rebellious. Whatever her parents did not want her to do was the thing she must do or die.

"Leo Keeler was also wild. She saw in him not only someone like herself, but someone so unlike her parents that they would be shocked when they found out she was sneaking out to see him, and she made sure they found out."

Tony and Keeler had been friends back then, and Tony knew that Leo was seeing a young girl from a good family, and that she sometimes spent the night in Leo's place down by the beach. Tony and Linda met, but they did not especially like one another. Toward the end of that summer, Linda had told Leo that she was pregnant, assuming she'd do the right thing by the standards of the time and marry her. Instead, he told her to tell her parents so they could pay for her to go to Mexico and have an abortion.

This was a dangerous and dirty business fifty years ago, Tony explained—a business of back-street doctors and fatal infections. It was also illegal, and a woman could go to prison for terminating a pregnancy. Her alternative would be to have the child out of wedlock and disgrace her family. Linda refused to tell her parents and told Leo he had to marry her. Instead, he kicked her out of his house. Tony found her that night down on the beach, crying.

"So you married her," I said.

"She needed someone. And I think also that I was even a worse slap in the face to her parents than Leo would have been. I stopped painting and went to work building roads, until I had saved enough money for us to live on while I painted again. We had only the one child, *mi hija,* Irene. I couldn't have loved her more."

And she repaid him with a lifetime of hate, taught to her by a mother who deserted them both. I didn't know what to say to him. His eyes were still dreaming into the past, moist with tears.

"So now you know why Leo hated me," he said, finally.

"He had nothing except a talent for making others despise him. I had everything he could have had, and threw away. I had a beautiful daughter, I had the love of my grandchildren, I had success in my career and standing in the town, and for a while I even had Linda."

"And he found a way, finally, to strike back, didn't he?"

"I believe he did, yes. I believe he did this to me." He held up his scarred hands. "And that is the reason the police think I killed him. They think I'm bitter, and they are partly right. I was bitter, and I thought my life was over, but that was just self-pity. I'm still alive, as anyone can see." He leaned closer to the mesh. "Do you know where David went today?"

I thought back to what Val had said. "To San Diego to buy art supplies."

"For me. I am going to try painting again."

This was the first good news I'd heard all day. "That's wonderful! I was afraid you'd given it up."

"I convinced myself that I must give it up, and so I did, after the hospital. It made me drink a lot, not being able to paint."

He held up his hands, layered in scars, the end joints of some of the fingers burned away. "My work will be different, cruder, but it will still be my work. I'll find a new style to suit my limitations. I'm not young anymore. I don't have a lifetime in front of me, as I did when I first came here. But an artist without art may as well be dead already. I've decided this. In three days I'll be out of this place, and trying to make up for the time I've wasted."

In three days he'd be out. I had to believe that, too. I had to put the pieces I'd been gathering together and try to come up with some new insights, or a new line of investigation. The police had Tony for the moment, and they weren't going to be sitting on their hands for the next three days; they were going to be working hard to keep him. What frightened me most was that I didn't have the slightest idea what to do about it.

CHAPTER 28

• • • • • • • • • • • • • •

I DROVE INLAND, TRYING TO GET AS FAR AWAY FROM THE sound of the ocean as possible. The road curved around sere, brown hills, past once-charming small towns with small-town names that were rapidly being devoured by the San Diego sprawl. I felt like rolling down my window and shouting a warning as I drove through, but who would listen?

I passed Escondido and kept driving, gaining altitude as I headed for Palomar, where I hadn't even known I was going. It seemed right, though, for my present needs—a dose of the mountains to counteract the relentless flatness of the beach and the infinite blue water.

It was all getting to be a bit much for me, and any resemblance this drive had to running away was not entirely coincidental. I had gassed up the car as I left Morado Beach, and now I was working on emptying it again as I pushed myself up the winding mountain roads at speeds that may have been less than totally safe, but felt therapeutic as hell. My tape player was broken, so I had only myself and my thoughts for company, and wouldn't you know it—those were the very things I wanted to run away from.

What I wanted—what I needed and couldn't have—was to close out all my accounts at the memory bank for a couple of days and not worry about anything like whether friends of mine were murderers, whether they might be going to jail for killing people who just possibly needed killing, whether they were living with terrible secrets, or just having their worlds turned inside out by uncaring circumstance. What I had was an overdose of unpleasant dead men and sympathetic suspects.

I found a high meadow ringed with pines and firs and took a pillow and a quilt out of the back of the car. I parked and walked until I found a spot close enough to a cluster of trees to stay in the shade for a couple of hours, and far enough from the road that all I could hear was the jays bitching at the squirrels. I took off my shoes and lay down and watched the clouds making fluffy Rorschach blots in the sky until I fell asleep.

When I came to, it was midafternoon. The sun had gone down below the tops of the trees across the meadow. I had lost perhaps three hours to unconsciousness, but gained, for the same period, the kind of forgetfulness that only sleep or death can provide. I suppose if I could have died for three hours, it would have accomplished the same purpose.

Back when I was married to Michael and my life was going nowhere, and my marriage going somewhere I didn't want to follow, I got in the habit of sleeping twelve or fourteen hours a day. I'd come home from work desperate for sleep more days than not, and fall into bed while the sun was still shining. In the morning I'd drag myself reluctantly out of bed, feeling like there was nothing I'd rather do than get back in and let the blackness have me again. Michael was seldom home, so he never noticed.

I'd gotten over that habit, like I got over smoking and a few others that weren't producing positive effects in my life— like Michael. I got over him, too, in the end, but there were times when a long nap for no purpose other than sheer escape still seemed called for. This one had made me ready to start driving downhill again, which was more than I could have hoped for.

I stopped for something to eat in a roadside café and took a table by a window. Without realizing it, I had my notebook out and was leafing through the pages when my cheeseburger arrived.

Stone was dead, damn him. He had started all this by getting in the way of a bullet one night last week, and that led to all the stupid little pages in the notebook, with all the stupid little scribbled notes.

If he would just stand up and say, "Hey, folks, I was only kidding," and go back to dealing dope and improving the community and abusing his wife, I could rip out all these pages and toss them in an authorized recycling receptacle like a good citizen, and stop suspecting people I knew of murder.

Of course, that still left Leo Keeler. Well, life just isn't simple, is it?

I went ahead and added Irene and Russ to the written list of Stone suspects, just to make it accurate. What was pissing me off was the fact that none of these people seemed to have killed either of these guys. That either meant I was incapable of suspecting anyone of committing murder, or I was missing a big bet somewhere.

Actually, Edmund Berenson seemed capable, just not stupid enough to off Stone under the circumstances. That could mean there were things between them I didn't know about yet that would make the circumstances different. Certainly the warehousing and sale of large quantities of hard drugs and the subsequent channeling of funds into legitimate investments might put a strain on a relationship. Maybe the clue lay in that aspect of their partnership.

I was still also rather fond of the professional assassin theory, mostly because it got me off the hook for gross incompetence, but also because it would leave just these kinds of tracks: no murderer and no weapon in evidence. It lacked the classic "gangland style" you read about in the papers, but who's to say these guys always like to advertise?

Leo Keeler could just as easily have been a victim of the same crowd if you bought the theory that he was some kind of drug middleman, but Rob had a lot of evidence against that. Just because something can be made to fit attractively into a theory doesn't mean you should get out a knife and trim the edges off.

Irene had been rejected by Stone, and she may have hated him enough to kill him; she certainly thought little enough of Tony not to care if he took the rap. Supposedly, she had been out of town on the night of the shooting, but I figured for something as important as first-degree murder, she could

always have made the trip. As far as I knew, though, she
hadn't had any association with Keeler in over forty years,
and certainly didn't know he was her father, not that that was
any kind of motive either.

Russ could have killed Stone to get Val back, and Val could
have killed him to keep Russ from finding out about the affair,
but neither of them had any reason to kill Keeler.

Brian and Andy McCain both had reason to hate Stone.
Barbara had even more. Maybe he *was* playing house with
the maid, and it had proved to be the last straw. Maybe, in
the absence of a butler, the maid did it herself.

David could have killed him for Tony, provided he knew
why Tony had threatened his life. And of course Tony could
have, and either or both of them could have killed Leo. And
let's not forget Crystal Kramer. She'd be crushed if I considered her too insignificant and dull to be a suspect. I took a
moment to think whether there was anyone I knew in the
entire world who might not be a reasonable suspect. I could
only come up with one, so I went outside to the pay phone
and called him.

"Still hanging in there, Burke?"

"Just barely, Jake. Actually, I've made loads of progress—it
just doesn't amount to shit, is all. My client has been arrested,
but I think he might be out on a habeas corpus in a couple of
days, but even if he is, he's not off the hook yet." I sighed,
feeling more like Jake's teenage daughter than a P.I. with a
license in my pocket. "And my emotional life is an accident
waiting to happen, and I keep finding out things I don't want to
know and would rather forget." There was silence on the other
end. "And I think I'm getting a blister on my left heel."

"Don't pop the blister. Wear a Band-Aid on it."

"How about the other stuff?"

"There are all kinds of Band-Aids, but they just put off the
inevitable. Actually, I can tell you're doing just fine; this is
only your second call in five days."

"You're right. I thought I'd be on the phone every fifteen
minutes."

"Well, if you really wanted me to solve your problems
for you, you probably would have been. You're a grown-
up, now."

Wow. Imagine me a grown-up, and only thirty-two. Jake filled me in on the latest news and gossip from Cascade, and I felt connected again. I even felt like driving back down to the coast.

Halfway there, I realized I had fled town before I told Rob about Lapierre Computer Systems. I considered calling him, but I didn't feel *that* good. It would be hard to separate our personal relationship from our professional differences, now that Tony was behind bars and Rob had put him there. I didn't want to see Rob until I had something that might help Tony. What I wanted right now was more dope on Edmund Berenson, and I had a feeling I knew right where to get it.

CHAPTER 29

· · · · · · · · · · · · · · ·

CRYSTAL KRAMER WAS A LOT LIKE HER NAME. ONE HAD TH[E]
feeling that if one hit her just right with a tiny hammer, sh[e]
would fragment into a million pieces. Crystal was the type o[f]
person of whom it is said that if you put a lump of coal u[p]
her ass, in three weeks you'd have a diamond.

Except for the fact that neither of us was remotely popula[r]
in school, we had absolutely nothing in common. We ha[d]
socialized occasionally—well okay, rarely—but enough tha[t]
I felt less than totally obvious calling her up and inviting he[r]
out for a drink.

"Oh, I don't drink, Caley. Thank you anyway."

"Well, are you doing something special tonight, Crys?" Sh[e]
had always liked being called Crys—it made her feel like on[e]
of the girls.

"Well, no. Not really."

"Then come out and watch *me* drink. You might get a laug[h]
out of it."

"I guess it won't hurt me to get away for a little while, bu[t]
I've got some extra work to catch up for Mr. Berenson. I'[ll]
meet you around eight. Where will you be?"

"Where's a good place for a couple of single girls to spen[d]
an evening where eight or ten appliance salesmen won't tr[y]
to hit on them?"

She named a place seven or eight eucalyptus-lined mile[s]
south of town, and we made a date.

176

I stopped by the gallery and visited with Val. She was feeling optimistic about Tony since she'd talked with Brian McCain, and I certainly wasn't going to shatter her mood. I made a mental note to stop by Brian's office first thing tomorrow and fill him in on what I had found out so far. I saw David standing in the next room, and went to talk with him.

"How bad is it, really?" was the first thing he wanted to know.

"I honestly can't say. If Tony wasn't anywhere near the crime scene, there won't be evidence that he was, and that's important. They've got some kind of circumstantial case, and they'll keep trying to add to it, while hoping for something better to come along. If they get enough, they'll try to go to court with it."

"And if they do get enough?"

"You need to talk to Brian McCain."

"I have. He's mad as shit, and wants Rob Cameron's ass." He watched me for reaction.

"Right now, I'd let him have it."

"This case has been hard on your personal life, hasn't it?"

I sighed. "Harder than most. It's okay, though. We'll work it out."

"You mean you and Rob?"

"I guess that's what I mean. Did you get to visit Tony today?"

"Yeah. He's worried for the first time since this whole thing started. He has a lot of faith in you, though, and in Brian. I think he believes he'll be out in a couple of days."

I just nodded, because although I hoped, too, I couldn't truly say that I believed.

When I left the gallery, I still had an hour before I was supposed to meet Crystal. I went back to the empty beach house and called Pat to see if he had any news on the Berenson fingerprint thing. I think I was hoping for good news, but that's not what I got.

"I can't find any record that those prints have come back yet, Ms. Burke. Seems like it wouldn't take this long—they do the comparisons by computer, and you can usually get a yes or no by the next day. I'll bet they're in, and nobody's given them to Sergeant Cameron yet. You have to remember, that was just a few hours before the explosion down on the pier, and since then things have been pretty crazy around the department. Two murders—Jesus, what a mess it's been. I'll bet it just got buried at the bottom of some pile on his desk. I'll be sure to have him ask about it tomorrow."

"Okay. Thanks, Pat. I really appreciate your help. Don't get yourself in any trouble about this, though."

"No, ma'am, I won't. But there's something more you ought to know. It's about Mr. Garza's case. Sergeant Cameron found dynamite on his property."

"Jesus." I sank into a nearby chair, suddenly having forgotten how to stand. They'd found the dynamite. "Where on his property? Do you know?"

"In a shed, they said. Just a couple of sticks. And after Mr. McCain came down to the station and they questioned Mr. Garza, he told them he'd done demolitions way back when. It doesn't prove anything, of course. . . ."

"No. It doesn't prove anything. But it doesn't help matters much, either. At least not from my point of view."

"No, ma'am, and what's more, I think Sergeant Cameron may be trying to prove that Mr. Garza killed Leo Keeler to keep Leo from incriminating him in some way about the Stone murder. It's all pretty sketchy, because the sergeant won't fill me in on anything anymore, but I heard him arguing with Keeler on the phone about a statement. I don't know what, exactly, but Sergeant Cameron mentioned it a couple of times. 'You're going to make that statement,' he said."

"Why are you telling me all this, Pat?"

"Because I can't figure out why Mr. Garza had to be arrested all of a sudden, on such flimsy evidence. It's like you said— he wasn't going anywhere. Something about it just bothers the hell out of me."

"Me, too."

I was pretty low by the time I hung up the phone. How could David have left two sticks of dynamite behind when he was so worried it would be found? However it had happened, something remained for Rob to find, and one more bone had been added to the skeleton of the case he was trying to build against Tony.

I dragged myself upstairs to change for my meeting with Crystal, and made myself hope that I could learn something important tonight—anything that would keep this day from being a total waste.

CHAPTER 30

. . . .

I HAD MADE A BET WITH MYSELF THAT CRYSTAL WOULD BE
right on time. I won. I also lost, of course, but I didn't let it
get me down. I had taken a window table looking out on the
front parking lot, and as soon as I saw her drive by looking
for a spot, I signaled the waitress and ordered a grasshopper,
hoping no one would witness my shame.

Crystal came in the bar and looked around at the tables full
of socializing singles, her hands tucked neatly in front of her
like a schoolgirl getting ready to read a book report. I waved
to her and she smiled gratefully and came over.

The waitress brought my drink and put a napkin down in
front of Crystal. "Can I get you something, ma'am?"

Although I was getting fed up with being called "ma'am"
every time I turned around since I turned thirty, I'd be willing
to bet that Crystal's old maid bearing had made everyone refer
to her like that since she was nineteen.

"Some orange juice, I think," she said with a little smile.

The waitress shrugged and started to walk back to the bar,
but I grabbed her sleeve.

"Do me a favor, Crys, and try what I'm having. Just a sip;
see what you think."

She took a dainty sip through the straw. Her eyes lit up.
"That's delicious! Is it alcoholic?"

"Barely," I promised. "Bring my friend another of those,

180

and I'll have a Bacardi Silver on the rocks with a lime wedge. Thanks." The waitress gave me a look, but went away to fill the order.

"This is a pretty upscale place," I commented. "Is this where successful young businessmen spend their evenings networking with their kind?"

"I've never been here," she confessed. "Mr. Berenson brings people here sometimes, though. I've heard him mention it." I observed—not for the first time—that Crystal took on a different look when she talked about Edmund Berenson; she was almost pretty. One thing for sure, there certainly weren't going to be any lonely appliance salesmen hitting up single women in any bar Edmund Berenson frequented, in either of his incarnations. I scooted my chair around to have a better view of the room. My handbag fell on the floor with a weighty clunk.

Crystal stared.

"Heavy makeup." I picked it up and placed it quietly on the table. "So I guess things have slowed down a bit at Stone and Berenson lately, hmm?"

"Not really. Mr. Berenson has a pretty heavy backlog of work, and he's taken on all Mr. Stone's files, too. There are still a lot of things for the lawyers to decide, and the will hasn't been read yet."

"Yes, I guess Barbara Stone will probably end up with Mr. Stone's share of the business. I hope that won't be bad news for Mr. Berenson."

She shook her head in the middle of a long sip of grasshopper. "He wouldn't let that affect his work with the company, anyway. He's very loyal."

There it was again, that barely perceptible glow whenever she mentioned Berenson's name. This girl was in love! I doubted a man who looked and moved like Edmund Berenson had to settle for the Crystal Kramers of the world in the sack, but I wondered if Berenson had taken the opportunity anyway.

Nope, I thought, as I watched her lowering the level of green froth in her glass, Crystal's love was definitely the unrequited kind, untouched by reality of any degree. Crystal certainly didn't know how lucky she was in that respect.

We spent the next two drinks reminiscing about high school,

a period in my life I'd sooner forget, except for the good times I had with Val, David, and Tony, and of course except for Rob. Crystal filled me in on the latest gossip—who was married to and/or divorced from whom. I let it all breeze past, making the occasional appropriate comment while waiting for Crystal to get drunker, and turning the case around in my head to try to get a better look at it.

"It must have been hell on you to miss the reunion," I commented sympathetically.

"Well, I see so many of those people here in town, you know. Even of all the ones who moved away, you'd be just amazed by how many have come back again."

No, I reflected, I probably wouldn't.

"Anyway, I was planning on being there, but Mr. Berenson called at the last minute and asked if I could make a trip down to Chula Vista for him."

My hand froze for an instant on its way to my glass, then I recovered long enough to take a hefty swallow of rum. "Really? What for?"

"Oh, there was some computer equipment he needed me to pick up. The place was supposed to be open late on Friday, but it wasn't, and I ended up having to wait while Mr. Berenson called someone to drive over from El Cajon and open up and give me the boxes."

"Little boxes? Are we talking RAM chips or what?"

"No, big boxes. Two computers and two monitors. They almost couldn't get it all in my car."

I gave a high sign to the waitress, who started over. "Would you like another one of those, Crys?"

She giggled. "Yes, I would, but I think you were fooling me about the alcohol."

"Maybe just a little." I pointed at the glasses, and the waitress nodded and headed back for the bar. "You're having fun, aren't you?"

"You know, I don't think I've had this good a time since high school." She smiled chummily.

I smiled back, feeling like a sewer rat, but this was getting hot, and I wasn't about to back down now for the sake of being a better person. "Do you go down to Chula Vista very often for the company?"

"Well, besides hardware, we also get all our forms and paper, disks, accessories, all that stuff from down there. Not just for our office, but a lot of the subsidiary businesses, too. Sometimes I can't believe how much stuff we get from them. Boxes and boxes. Sometimes Mr. Berenson goes himself, but often as not I run down in the company van and save him the trouble. He's so busy, and he works so hard." Her face went all mushy again.

"He must be getting a pretty good price to go so far out of his way."

"Yes, they give us a great discount, but we're outside their delivery area. I wish they had a warehouse closer to Morado Beach."

"You know, Val told me she's been looking for a place to buy a new computer system. Maybe I could pass the name of the place on to her." I waited for this to sink in; Crystal was on her third grasshopper, and a little green mustache was decorating her upper lip. I decided not to tell her, and she could enjoy it later.

"Yes, I'm sure she'd get a good deal there. It's called Lapierre."

Mais naturellement. I slipped my notebook out of my bag and pretended to make a note of it.

"Exchanging shopping tips, ladies?" The deep, cultured voice over my shoulder could only belong to one man.

"Oh, Mr. Berenson!" Crystal exclaimed breathlessly. "You've met Caley Burke. She's an old friend of mine from high school."

I willed my face to unfreeze and turned around to meet him, trying to slide the notebook back into my handbag without letting Berenson have a peek at my Walther. "How nice to see you again," I gushed. "Crys said you recommended this place. It's terrific." I gestured at all the yuppie ambience.

He took my hand in a warm, firm grasp of the kind recommended to people who want to be known as forthright and sincere. "It's a pleasure seeing you again. May I join you two for a drink?" He sat down in the third chair without waiting for confirmation. The waitress was at the table in fifteen seconds, bringing our round and Berenson's usual.

"This," Crystal said, pointing to the minty foam in her glass, "is a grasshopper, and I swear I never had anything that tasted so good. Caley got me to try it, but now I think I'm getting a little drunk."

"Well, sometimes it's good to let go of our inhibitions a bit, Crystal. Enjoy." He raised his own drink to her, then turned and met my eyes over the rim of his glass. The look was cold and hard, but there was a touch of pallor under the tan. I kicked myself for being stupid enough to tip him off.

I took a stiff drink of my rum and looked at my watch. Mickey's little yellow hands were a blur in my state of anxiety. "Oh, my gosh, look at the time! I promised Val I'd help her move some stuff down at the gallery. I'd better run. Thanks for the conversation, Crys. It was nice seeing you again, Mr. Berenson."

"Call me Ed. I'll get this round, Ms. Burke. Drive safely."

"Not a problem," I said. I didn't know how wrong I'd turn out to be.

CHAPTER 31

. . . .

I WAS A COUPLE OF MILES AWAY AND PROCEEDING LAWFULLY
toward Morado Beach, on account of the drinks I'd had, when
I saw the headlights coming up behind me like a streak. Some
jerks just have to let you know you aren't going fast enough
to suit them.

I started increasing my speed, trying to keep the guy off my
tail, but he stuck to me like bubble gum. When I looked down
at the speedometer, I was pushing seventy-five. I decided I
didn't need to drive this fast just to prove anything to this
guy. I slowed down and pulled toward the shoulder, giving
him some extra room to get around.

"Okay, I give up," I said. "Come on and pass me." What
happened instead sobered me up in a flash.

The car, a large American-made sedan with an unfair advantage in the mass department over my little Japanese hatchback,
rammed my rear bumper, hard. "Jesus!" I shouted, fear giving
rise to adrenaline, and that in turn slowing down the next few
seconds to a tortuous crawl.

I felt my wheels lose traction, and then my car veered left
across the road, toward a row of sturdy old eucalyptus that
formed a barrier between the northbound and southbound lanes
of the highway. I remembered, crazily, how every now and
again a campaign would be mounted to get rid of the trees,
usually right after some hapless driver had pulped himself

against one of them when he fell asleep at the wheel. Or was run off the road?

I could see the shaggy brown and white bark of the eucalyptus, peeling downward in little strips, just in front of my windshield. I pulled the wheel hard to the right and the back of the car came around and slammed into the trunk of the tree. There was a brief moment of utter silence. I was scared shitless to look back at the other car, for fear I would see it looming in the side window, bearing down on me.

I righted the wheel and hoped the left rear tire would still turn, then reached down and popped the four-wheel drive lever up and shoved the gearshift into first. Gunning the engine, I threw up a rooster tail of dirt and gravel as I fought to regain the pavement. My eyes went to the rearview mirror. The sedan was still behind me, waiting. Shit.

It didn't enter my mind for a second that this could have been an accident; I guess I'm just naturally paranoid. I could see a couple of choices, and I didn't have much hope for either of them. One was to try to outrun the bigger car. On a winding road, this would be a possibility, if I could outdrive him. On a straight highway he had a clear advantage in horsepower.

My other choice was to leave the car and try to get away on foot. I had no idea whether I could outrun this joker, or if he might be armed. I knew I didn't have much chance of outrunning a bullet. I slammed down the four-wheel lever, put my right foot down hard, and took the easy way out. I felt a glimmer of hope as the speedometer needle rolled over toward the bottom peg, even though in this car that wasn't particularly fast.

I scanned the highway for a black-and-white. Surely someone would notice all this murderous activity and alert the highway patrol. At the very least, I could get pulled over for speeding. It would be the first time I'd looked forward to it.

As I'd feared, the sedan was back on my tail in seconds. I felt the awful jarring sensation again, this time aware of the pain from my already abused muscles. I really didn't need this.

The universe went into slow motion once more. Because of this, I had plenty of time to turn the wheel again, but this time it only saved me from taking another tree totally head-on. My left front fender took the brunt, and my head smacked into the steering wheel as I was thrown hard against my seat belt. God bless my seat belt.

I think it may have been a few seconds before I was able to make another attempt to get out of there. Still in molasses time, I shifted into first and pressed down on the accelerator. Nothing. The engine had died. I started it up, hoping it was drivable. I never found out.

Something struck the window by my head, over and over. The window caved in in a shower of glass chunks and glass shards and sparkling glass dust. A hand reached out of the dark beyond the car, grabbed the door handle, and opened it; another hand reached in the opening and grabbed me by the hair. Edmund Berenson reached over and unfastened my seat belt, one hand still tangled in my hair. He pulled, and I came up out of the seat, offering very little resistance. I did manage to grab my handbag by the strap on my way out. He didn't seem to notice.

"How about a late-night swim?" he inquired in that sexy voice. He opened the passenger door of the sedan, which looked a little worse for wear about the front bumper. For people like me, that would be incriminating, all those paint streaks and such, but I had no doubt he had ways of getting around that.

As I wondered idly about this, it occurred to me that I might be in a slight state of shock. I felt devoid of reflexes, and wasn't sure if I'd be able to summon the speed to help myself out of this situation before he could stop me.

At least I could be prepared for it down the road, I told myself, though I hadn't the slightest notion when or if that opportunity might present itself. As he turned his head to check the traffic, I slipped the strap of my bag over my head, so that it would stay with me. That was all I had to give it right now.

We drove the rest of the way into town, and north to Irene's, where he parked on the road well out of the illumination from the porch light. A few times on the way I had thought I saw headlights behind us, but they always turned off. No help there. He pulled me out of the car and steered me up to the house. The lights were out and the driveway was empty. No one was home, as usual.

"Use your key and open the door," he told me.

I did. My mind was still asleep at the wheel, though beginning to clear slightly, and I felt terribly weak. We walked into the dark house and I fumbled for the hall light and switched it on.

He waved the gun toward the stairs. "Now we're going up to your room and you're going to change into your swimsuit."

"I don't even own a swimsuit," I told him. "I don't swim, and everyone who knows me knows that." I wasn't so rummy I couldn't tell what he had in mind for me. I must be feeling better.

"Well, people do crazy things when they're drunk, don't they?" He pulled me over to the liquor cabinet and took out a bottle of vodka.

Irritation took over for part of my fear. I hate vodka. "Jesus, Ed, you're about to drown someone who never goes near the water, and you've left a wrecked car by the side of the highway. This is a pretty spur-of-the-moment thing with you, isn't it? You must not be used to doing your own dirty work."

His face twitched once, and he backhanded me into the dining-room table with his gun hand. There was a white flash of pain as the skin on my cheekbone split open. I fell against the edge of the table and down onto the floor, dragging a chair down with me. If I could get past the pain, I thought, this might be a good time to see if I could get my bag open and get to my gun. I fumbled with the catch and it opened, but he snatched me back up to my feet before I could reach inside. "Come on," he said, and his voice didn't sound sexy anymore.

We headed into the kitchen and out the back door. Today's batch of sun tea was still sitting out on the deck railing, and I sure wished I could take it inside before it soured. He kept me in front of him as we made our way down the steps. I stumbled in the soft sand below the stairs, and left my shoes behind.

The ocean roared; the same crowd-goes-mad muffled cry over and over again that you can never take meaning from no matter how many times you hear it. A nearly full moon was just coming up over the hills as the last of the daylight faded into the water. I wanted, irrationally, to concentrate on this sort of natural beauty, seeing as how it might be the last time, but the deadly presence of the gun kept my wandering mind in check.

You won't die, I began telling myself as I stumbled down the beach. No matter what happens here, you won't die.

I can't say now whether I ever believed it.

When we were about a hundred yards from the house, he stopped and pushed me down onto the wet sand. He uncapped the vodka and handed it to me. "Drink this." He was pointing the gun at me in a meaningful way.

I took the bottle. "I really don't understand why you're doing this."

"Don't you, Miss Barton? I said drink."

I tilted the bottle up and took a drink. Irene's vodka was undoubtedly the best available, but even the best vodka is still pretty vile. I tried letting very little go down my throat and a whole lot go down my neck. There was quite a bit of light from the moon, but Berenson was standing seaward of me, and if I faced the surf, the light would all be behind me, and should make me harder to see. I scooted around slightly to do so. "I don't know anybody named Barton," I told him.

"Don't you? She was down in Chula Vista last night snooping around. With her brother. Do you have a brother, Ms. Burke?"

God, don't let him go after Andy. I was praying to something I haven't believed in since childhood, but I wasn't going to leave any bases uncovered now.

"Keep drinking—I want plenty of alcohol in your bloodstream."

"A drunk in the water is a dead drunk," a cop told me one time. He was the head of the Lake Patrol up in Cascade, and if they paid him even a modest bounty for every floater he pulled out of that lake in the summer, he could retire inside three years.

In my case it was probably moot, since I swim with all the alacrity of a rock. My resolve to get out of this somehow hardened up just a bit more. I did my drinking act again, and choked a bit, partly for effect, partly because I was actually swallowing some. "Let me slow down a little. If I throw it up, it won't be in my bloodstream anyway." He raised his eyes to the landward horizon, scanning. Maybe I could prolong this long enough for someone to come home and notice the classic signs of struggle we'd left behind in the house. "You must have broken glass all over that nice suit. Doesn't that worry you at all?"

"No. It doesn't. Have another drink. You know, you should have known better than to question my secretary. Eventually, she tells me everything."

I had another moment of fear that had nothing to do with my present predicament. "You didn't hurt Crystal, did you?"

"Crystal doesn't know shit, which is why she's so handy for moving merchandise. If you were as stupid as Crystal, you'd be safe in bed right now."

Not for the first time, I wished myself unburdened by the ravages of intelligence.

His eyes kept darting up to the house, as though he had seen something. I sincerely hoped he had. My hand inched toward the flap on my bag, which had fallen behind me on its strap. I kept my other hand busy with the bottle, hoping to keep his attention on that. He lowered the gun for a moment and cocked his head, trying to hear something above the sound of the waves. I got my hand all the way inside the bag, and my fingers were closing on something when I heard a shout.

"All right, Berenson, this is the police. Put down your gun, and step away!"

CHAPTER 32

. . . .

A LOOK OF PUZZLEMENT CROSSED BERENSON'S PERFECT FACE. He started to walk toward the voice, gun in hand. A gun flashed and barked from the darkness, and he went flying back toward the surf and was perfectly still. I threw down the bottle and scrambled to my feet.

Rob came running down the beach toward me, holstering his gun. "Are you all right?"

I clung to him and shook, finally free to give in to fear. He held me and stroked me and murmured comforting things, but there was still a dead man a few feet behind me, and I'd been very close to being dead myself. "How did you know . . ."

"I didn't. I just came by to see if you were here, and saw his car. You left the front door standing open, and there was a chair knocked down in the dining room. I looked out back and saw the two of you out on the beach."

He let go of me and walked over to the body. In the moonlight, the blossoming stain on Berenson's shirtfront looked shiny black, like oil. I shuddered. I haven't seen that many dead people in my life, and I keep hoping each one is the last.

Rob knelt down and pressed his fingers into the side of Berenson's throat for a few seconds, then shook his head. He picked up the gun with his handkerchief and put it in his jacket pocket.

My head was still spinning, and I was buzzed on adrenaline and beginning to realize that in spite of my trick on Berenson, I had swallowed more vodka than I thought. I wanted to tell Rob everything right then. When the shock wore off and the pain set in, I was going to crash hard, and I figured I'd earned it. "That isn't all, Rob. That isn't nearly all. He ran me off the road. Oh, shit, my car. My car is totaled, too. What a week."

"Are you all right? Are you hurt?" His eyes scanned my face anxiously.

My hand went up to the new bump on my forehead— inches from the stitches that were my souvenir of Leo Keeler's demise—then to the trickle of blood from my cheek. Rob took a clean handkerchief from his jacket and held it to the cut.

"He was going to kill me," I told him. "I found out about Chula Vista. God." I took the handkerchief and swabbed at my cheek. This was definitely going to scar. Great. The landward night breeze began to stiffen, raising goose bumps on my arms. I took Rob's hand and started pulling him toward the house. "I need to get inside—I'm freezing."

Rob stopped in his tracks. "What are you talking about, Caley?"

"Chula Vista. A warehouse." I turned back toward the warmth and safety of the house, and started walking without him. "Hauling drugs up here in computer boxes. I had the goods on him."

He took a couple of long strides to catch up with me, then stopped me and turned me around, holding my shoulders. "Can you prove any of it?"

"I've been there. I'll give you the address. He must have killed Stone, too, or had someone else do it." Now the pieces that had resisted me so stubbornly began to click into place. "You see, Berenson wasn't on the run from the guys in L.A. He wouldn't have lasted this long. He had to be in cahoots with them. Maybe he was watching Stone for them, and Stone got greedy. Or maybe he just decided to take over from Stone, and they supported him."

Rob put an arm around my shoulders and drew me close to him. "Okay, okay. That's enough detective work for one night.

Let the police put all this stuff together. If it was one of the L.A. families, they'll find the trail goes cold anyway, long before it gets to anyone important. Right now it's time for you to get some rest and get over the shock you've been through. And we need to do something about that cut, too. Just let it go for a while."

We walked together up toward the house, but I couldn't let it go. For one thing, Tony was still in jail. For another, everything I'd ever thought or heard about this case was rushing through my mind at high speed, and I felt I had to make some sense of it.

"I still don't know who could have killed Keeler," I said to Rob. "It wasn't someone who knew much about explosives."

"It wasn't?"

"Nope. They used too much. Someone wanted him out of the way, though. Wait!" I stopped.

Rob tugged on my hand. "Wait for what? I thought you were cold."

"Now I'm red-hot. Rob, why couldn't Leo Keeler have been the one hauling the drugs? He could have brought them as far as San Diego, and then Stone and Berenson could have warehoused them in Chula Vista for as long as they wanted."

I was rolling now, punch drunk as hell and quite proud of myself. "You said his trips never coincided with an increase in the drug supply. Well, they wouldn't have to, would they? All he was doing was hauling it into the country. The boys from L.A. were taking care of the rest. And suppose after Stone was gone, Leo became a liability—what if he knew Berenson shot Stone and threatened to tell someone about it? Berenson would have had to get rid of him."

"Caley, enough already. You don't have to work overtime on this. You're probably still in shock, for God's sake. Let's go up to the house and call the station. Let the police take care of it."

I was suddenly very angry about the whole thing. "The police have *been* taking care of it, Rob, and they haven't done shit, except to arrest an innocent man. Someone greased Stone and Keeler, and it has nothing to do with Tony Garza, and everything to do with the drug supply all up and down this part of the coast. Just because you've got someone in custody, are you going to ignore evidence that's right in front of your eyes?"

I turned and pointed back at the crumpled form of Edmund Berenson on the dark sand, little wavelets venturing toward his hair like tentative fingers. "Berenson didn't try to kill me because he didn't like my looks. He tried to kill me because I was onto something. He panicked. He was more afraid of someone bigger than him finding out he'd blown chunks on this Lapierre thing than he was of leaving incriminating evidence all over the place."

I glared up at him. "Am I getting through to you?"

Rob looked back toward Berenson and nodded. "I'll bet you're right." He chuckled softly, shook his head. "I'll bet that's pretty much what happened. Berenson killed them both. He and Stone must have been running shit up and down the coast for years, with Leo's help, and Berenson must have decided he wanted it all."

"Does this mean you'll drop the charges against Tony?"

"Of course. Garza's free to go. We've got our man, and we've got you to thank for it." He smiled down at me. He seemed really happy for the first time, I realized, since I'd been back. The stress and pressure of the past week seemed to have dropped from him all at once.

He pulled me close to him. "I want you to marry me, Caley. I want us to go away from here and live the kind of life we've only dreamed about. Maybe we'll go out of the country. You don't have to say anything now—we'll talk about it when you've had time to recuperate."

"Yeah. Recuperate. What a vacation." I leaned against Rob, thankful for the solidity of his presence; thankful I wasn't as dead as old Ed back there. "Most people go see performing dolphins—I get kidnapped at gunpoint. Not to mention getting blown off the Seaside Pier." I put my arms around him, shivering slightly. "God, that was awful. You weren't there—you can't know."

Rob drew me close. "I would have been at the hospital with you if I could, babe. I told you, I was out of town. I didn't even know about the explosion until I called Pat."

"No, Rob, don't you remember? You told Pat you'd already heard about the explosion. Then he told you I was one of the people down on the pier."

"That's right. I remember now. I was just so afraid for you. Let's get you into the house, and into bed. I'll stay with you until we can reach Val or Russ."

"Okay." We started walking again. "So did Pat tell you about the explosion, or did you already know?"

"What does it matter? You've had a bump on the head, and it's got you confused."

"You're right—I *am* confused. I was that night, too. Pat was there with me, in the emergency room. He said you called him and told him you'd heard about the explosion. . . ."

"Caley, will you please just leave it alone?"

"Then you told me you didn't know about the explosion." Little incidents were coming back again, like snapshots viewed at high speed. A hard knot of anxiety was making me sick at my stomach. "And you told me you hadn't spoken to Leo in ten years, but Pat said you'd talked to him on the phone the day he died."

"Caley, shut up!"

I stepped back from him. He was trembling. "You weren't out of town at all, were you? Unless maybe you were somewhere between the Seaside Pier and Chula Vista. They got away with it for so long because they had police protection, didn't they?"

"Sweetheart, listen to me. Stone and Keeler and Berenson were all slime, and they're all dead. Dead men don't hire lawyers. I can show good cause to wrap up this investigation, hang both raps on Berenson, and let Tony Garza go free. No one is going to be eager to look too hard for another perpetrator."

"Another perpetrator? Does that mean there is another one? Did *you* kill them?"

"It doesn't matter who killed them—it matters who the police and the D.A. can be made to think killed them. Think about it, Caley—we can go anywhere we want, do anything we want. There won't be anything out of reach for us anymore."

"There never were any stocks from your parents, were there? It's all drug money, and you've just been biding your time until you had everyone out of the way, so you could start spending it free and clear." Any semblance of mental fog had dissipated, and for just a moment I wished it back. I could feel my dream crumbling.

Rob had practically confessed to killing Stone and Keeler, I realized. Even Berenson's death, which looked like self-defense on the surface, had probably just been Rob covering his tracks, like always. Funny, but I couldn't feel the place my heart had been only moments before. All I wanted was to nail him to the wall. I wanted that admission, that confession, but how was I going to get it? He had fooled me this long—fooled everyone, for that matter. Who was I to think I could wrap up this case now, after the half-assed job I'd done so far?

"Caley, none of that is true—you've got to believe me!" I heard the fear in his voice. He put out a hand toward me; it trembled like a leaf.

The pressure was back, in spades, and all I had to do was keep it on. I'd be goddamned if I'd let Rob Cameron get away with murdering three people and my dreams. He was truly rattled now, and if I could keep him off balance, I just might get my confession after all. I couldn't give him a chance to regroup.

"It's no use, Rob, I know you were the key to Stone's whole operation. I know you've been moving shit through L'Auberge . . ." He flinched at that one, which had been barely more than a lucky guess, and I decided to tip him a little further. It was a dangerous lie, but everything might be riding on it. " . . . and I have a witness."

"You're full of shit," he said, but he didn't believe it. "Who?"

"Pat. He's been suspicious for a long time of the way you've kept him in the dark, and decided to do a little investigating on his own. He told me everything."

"Caley, why didn't you just let it be?" Rob's voice carried a terrible sadness. I reached out my hand to him, but his arm shot out and grabbed me. "I just wanted you to stop thinking about it—let it go. It would have been all right." He started pulling me down the beach, away from the house. I knew right away where he was heading, and I didn't want to go there.

"Why Keeler, Rob?" I struggled to keep my footing in the sand and hoped I wouldn't trip over a rock. "What made Keeler dangerous enough to kill?"

"He killed Stone. He dressed up like Garza and stood out on the sidewalk in plain sight and shot him. It wasn't that late—I figured on witnesses. I told Leo if he didn't do Stone, I'd tell Berenson he was the guy some greasers in L.A. were looking for from fifty years ago. The old bastard was too fucking stupid to know the people he pissed off down there haven't been anybody since the big East Coast families moved west after the war."

"Keeler was working for you the whole time?"

"I had him by the short hairs. I told him Stone and Berenson were some of the guys looking for him, and I'd take care of him—make sure they didn't find him. He was scared shitless of them. I gave him enough to keep him in booze, and he thought he was lucky." He slowed down as he got into the story, and I was grateful for the time.

"We went through Garza's house while they were both gone one night. We took the gun and some other shit, and I told him if he used the gun to shoot Stone, I'd put Garza away for it. Finding the dynamite was a coincidence. I didn't take it—I didn't know I'd need it."

"So Keeler shot Stone for you? Because of some lie you told him?"

"Yeah, and then he went out and got falling-down drunk. He disappeared for a couple of days, and when he came back, he told me he'd gotten rid of the gun. I told him he had to make a statement—say that he saw Garza shoot Stone. He wouldn't do it. I knew I couldn't count on him anymore; he wasn't as afraid of me as he was of God punishing him for the things he'd done to Garza."

"Then he *did* set the fire in Tony's studio."

"He says he did. The insurance investigation couldn't prove it, and I didn't want him going to jail for it. I needed him to keep bringing the shit in."

"So the gun was supposed to frame Tony?"

"Once it got too late to use the chemical tests that could prove he hadn't fired a gun recently. The gun was going to turn up in a Dumpster somewhere, wiped clean. We were

going to plant the rest of the stolen goods back in Garza's
house, and we were going to have a case. Leo fucked it up
but good. That's when I thought of the dynamite. I took some
from the evidence room and did Leo. Later I could call another
search of Garza's place, and there it would be."

And two officers did make a search, but by then the dynamite had been gone.

"I didn't know you'd be on the pier." He turned and looked
at me with what seemed like genuine sorrow. "I never meant
to hurt you.

"Once I had Garza in jail, I knew he'd never get out again.
In fact, by my calculations, Garza will have hanged himself
before another twenty-four hours are up. Dead men make great
perpetrators; ask the Warren Commission."

God, it was all so neat, and so deadly. A tidy little package
of death. Now, all he had to do was get rid of some loose
ends, like me. And Pat. Now Pat was in danger because I'd
lied to get a confession out of Rob. I had my confession, but
unless I could stop Rob, the cost would be too high.

We were getting closer and closer to the cave. Rob was
holding me by my left arm, already bruised from Berenson's
tender attentions. That left my right arm free, and my bag
was hanging on my right side. Normally I don't do anything
of importance with my right hand, but it looked like I might
have to make an exception. Unfortunately, I could think of no
foolproof way to reach into it and find my gun among all the
other junk in there without attracting Rob's attention, and I
was only going to get one chance. Reluctantly, I decided to
wait and see if it would present itself.

"Garza could be made to look as good for Leo as for Stone,"
Rob was saying. "He was sure Leo had set the fire—he might
have wanted to kill him for all anybody knew, and he had all
that dynamite. All I had to do was seize it in a search, and he
could be down for Leo, too."

"Only you couldn't find the dynamite. You had to go back
and plant some."

"Do you know where it is?" He turned his head toward me
and his eyes made my insides cold.

I looked away. "No," I said, truthfully enough. "I don't.
So why did Stone have to die in the first place?" I found

myself suppressing a giggle that almost certainly stemmed from oncoming hysteria. Here we were, taking a moonlight stroll on the beach while discussing cold-blooded murder—Stone, Keeler, Berenson—do we have a fourth? Let's see if Caley can play.

"It was my operation to begin with," Rob was saying. "There was just me and some other guys on the force running interference, and Leo bringing the stuff in. Stone found out about it while he was trying to set up his own operation. He gave me a choice: work for him and take a smaller cut, or get cut out entirely. I've been taking his nickles and dimes for the past seven years, waiting for my chance. Then Berenson clued me in that Stone had decided to have me taken care of. He didn't trust me anymore."

"Why did Berenson tell you?"

"You were right about him. He was watchdogging Stone for the L.A. heavies, and Stone was having him falsify the profit figures that were going back to them. So Berenson waited until he knew Stone was going to be alone in his office, and then he called me."

"Did you send Berenson after me?"

"No. My guess is he panicked when he found out you knew about the warehouse, and decided he had to kill you."

"I may be splitting hairs, but what are *you* planning?"

He shook his head, as though I were missing a simple point. "Yesterday I thought we could go away together—someplace where we could just live and not let any of this touch us. If you never knew the money didn't come from my parents' estate, you'd be happy with it." He looked toward the cliffs, moving a few steps this way and that, until he spotted the rock that marked the cave mouth; then we headed toward the tiny crack in the cliff. Still holding my arm, he felt for the opening.

"We still could be, Rob. I don't care where the money came from. Let's just leave this place." I hoped the desperation I felt was not leaking into my voice. I had a sickening vision of my body, wedged between rocks, floating gently in the waves.

He found the cave mouth, and pulled me inside. We headed toward the back, where the space between the walls began to narrow sharply. "Don't try to bullshit me, Caley. I know better, and so do you." It was black inside, and I kept cutting my feet

on the rocks that littered the cave floor. Rob didn't seem to
notice.

When the passage grew too narrow to walk side by side, he
stopped and pushed me up against the wall. "I'm not going
down for this," he said. "Not for anybody; not even you. I
looked for an opportunity like this from the time I joined the
force. You think I wanted to be a stupid cop all my life like
my dad, feeding bourbon to a stomach ulcer and dying of a
heart condition at fifty-three? Not a fucking chance. I worked
hard to get here."

And killed. And would kill again. He let go of me and
turned away with his head down. His breathing was ragged.
He reached into his inside pocket and pulled out a pack of
cigarettes. A match flared in the darkness.

My right arm inched toward my handbag while I took inven-
tory, trying to think of anything that would clank or rustle. My
fingers closed on steel. I bit back a sigh of relief and took the
gun out of the bag. Any sounds must have been covered by
the waves, because he just stood there and smoked.

The plan was to transfer the gun to my left hand, and wound
him. If I could bring him down, I could get away up the beach.
The Walther was only a .32, but the silvertip loads I kept in it
made a big hole, and even a flesh wound should cause enough
hydrostatic shock to bring him down for a minute or so. I could
live with that; I knew this beach and how to get off it.

He raised his head and turned. I lowered my hand. The
cigarette dropped with a hiss onto the wet sand.

Rob pressed me to the wall with his body. "I wanted you,
Caley. You'll never know how much." There was such tender-
ness in his voice that for half a second I was almost convinced
he didn't mean to kill me after all.

"Rob, please don't do this."

"I don't want to hurt you, Caley, but I tried, you know that.
You know how hard I tried to make it different for us."

He kissed me then, and my mind recoiled. Not like this,
Rob, I begged him silently. Don't make me do it like this. I
felt his right arm move up toward his jacket pocket, the one
where he had put Berenson's gun. So Berenson would get
the blame, I thought. Rob was always good at covering his
tracks.

I brought my right arm up, clumsy as it felt with that weight hanging from it.

He put his lips to my ear and whispered my name as he brought the gun close to my head.

I held the gun an inch from his left side, just under his arm, and pulled the trigger once, twice. He crumpled without a sound. I was grateful for that.

CHAPTER 33

• • • • • • • • • • • • • •

I WALKED UP THE BEACH IN THE GRAYISH-PALE MOONLIGHT that was almost like day, past Berenson's body, which didn't look, somehow, as though it had ever been a living person. My ears rang unpleasantly. Real life was really nothing like the pistol range, I thought numbly—no safety precautions whatsoever.

At the bottom of the steps I found my shoes, and carried them up to the deck, where I sat until Val came some time later and found me. She took the gun out of my hand and called David, then she wrapped me in blankets and laid me on Irene's red velvet sofa and made a fire. None of it could stop my shaking.

"Call the Sheriff's Department," I told her. "I think they're okay." She didn't know what I meant, but she did it anyway; then she cleaned and bandaged my feet.

When the deputies got there, I told them about the body outside on the beach. Then I told them how to find the cave, and what was in it, and why.

Fate—or whatever—had not granted my wish, but I had a lot to be thankful for. I was alive, and Tony would be released from jail, and except for the bouts of "what if" and "if only" that I knew I would play against myself for some time to come, it was finally all over.

When the sheriffs had gone for the night, David put me to

202

bed and lay there next to me in case I had bad dreams. When I did, he held me and told me everything was going to be all right. I believed him, because I had to believe something.

The next day was a nightmare of questions and answers. I drank coffee and stared out at the water while I gave statements about everything I had seen, heard, and done. I didn't mention the dynamite—I couldn't see how it mattered now. Val and David and Andy stayed in the house all day, looking after me, and now and again I saw Russ hovering, looking concerned. Irene had fled to the safety of a shopping jaunt to Newport Beach. Pat came by, and even Crystal, fragile with grief for Berenson, but holding her head high. I was inordinately glad to see her; I figured I must be getting sentimental. Somewhere in there, someone called Jake and told him I would be all right.

There would be a big investigation, they told me, into the workings of the Morado Beach Police Department, to determine just how far the corruption went that had allowed Stone and Berenson and Rob and Leo Keeler to do business unobstructed for seven years.

I thought a lot about the secret Tony had entrusted me with. Much as I didn't need another one, it was safer with me than with anyone. I couldn't take Tony away from Val and David and replace him with Leo Keeler. The only person who might be made any happier by such a revelation would be Irene, and I really didn't care that much.

When I couldn't pretend it hadn't happened any longer, I thought about Rob. There was less grief than I'd anticipated, and more guilt. When I could finally separate the fantasy from the reality, I could see that the person I'd wanted Rob to be and the person he actually was never really even knew each other, but it all came down to a single fact: a man was dead, and I'd killed him—not a stranger, but someone who had once meant a great deal to me. There was no Band-Aid for that. I had been forced to face the fact, and I would be forced to get on with life anyway, and I knew that eventually I would.

When night came again, David was still there. "Won't Tony be worried about you?" I asked him.

"Tony knows why I'm here," he said. I looked up at him, standing over my chair, looking at me, and I knew, too. I reached out for his hand and pulled him down to me.

That night there were no nightmares.

Saturday was a little easier, a little more like living in the real world, and Sunday I called Jake.

"I want you to take another week, Burke. You didn't have much of a vacation."

"I'm not sure I could survive another week like the last one, Jake."

"This one will be different. I promise. If anybody in that town kills anybody else during the rest of your vacation, I'll come down there personally and kick their ass. Besides, I have a couple of interesting cases here, and I want you to be in shape to handle them."

"All right. You talked me into it. Have I ever won an argument with you?"

"Absolutely not."

"Hey, I'm having my portrait painted. What do you think of that?"

"I think you'd better keep your clothes on; you know how artists are."

I smiled at David, who was standing by his easel, brush in hand, waiting for me to get back to my chair. "Oh, I do, Jake," I said, "I certainly do."